THE
PITCHFORK PATROL

**Center Point
Large Print**

**This Large Print Book carries the
Seal of Approval of N.A.V.H.**

THE
PITCHFORK PATROL

Will Henry

CENTER POINT PUBLISHING
THORNDIKE, MAINE

This Center Point Large Print edition
is published in the year 2007 by arrangement with
Golden West Literary Agency.

Copyright © 1962 by Henry Wilson Allen.
Copyright © renewed 1980 by Henry Wilson Allen.

All rights reserved.

The text of this Large Print edition is unabridged. In other
aspects, this book may vary from the original edition. Printed in
Thailand. Set in 16-point Times New Roman type.

ISBN-10: 1-58547-008-9
ISBN-13: 978-1-58547-008-8

Library of Congress Cataloging-in-Publication Data

Henry, Will, 1912-1991.
  The Pitchfork patrol / Will Henry.--Center Point large print ed.
    p. cm.
  Originally published under the pseudonym Clay Fisher.
  ISBN-13: 978-1-58547-008-8 (lib. bdg. : alk. paper)
  1. Large type books. I. Fisher, Clay, 1912-1991. Pitchfork patrol. II. Title.

PS3551.L393P58 2007
813'.54--dc22

2007004125

a long time late
for
James A. Pabian
who started
it all

HISTORICAL NOTE

The account which follows is based on an actual event. While, in the necessary bridgings-over of the missing sequences it will probably become more story than history, the bow to the record must still be made. In the beginning, there was such a mission and such a patrol and such an old cavalry sergeant.

Schlonager was not his real name, of course, nor was Fort Pitchfork the real name of his duty post. The Big Horn River and the Greybull and Tensleep basins and Gooseberry Creek and Cottonwood Creek and the spot where Fort McKinney stood are still there—or were the last time we saw Wyoming—and a few more places and names encountered in this report of the Pitchfork Patrol will be found by old-timers to stir a memory. But Schlonager and Scortini and Mudcat Clevenger and Casimir Pulaski and Ira Shank and the others of that ill-omened scout force are names not on the duty rosters of any cavalry garrison out there in that sweltering August of 1877.

As for the woman and what took place between her and Sergeant Schlonager the same immunity holds. Her name was surely not Dulcie Shuffman and her sod-house homestead was not staked on Gooseberry Creek at its confluence with the Big Horn River above Greybull. Yet little else has been shrouded in this telling of an old Wyoming tale. Its people lived. They did these things, and died or disappeared. What does it matter how they spelled their names?

Will Henry

WIND RIVER RESERVATION
1961

In Old Wyoming the Wind blows
Free
It wanders Forever and Will not be
Held in the Hand of any but me
And maybe, my friend, if you will
Listen
But thee. . . .

Anon.

THE
PITCHFORK PATROL

1

IT TOOK A TALL HORSE TO CARRY HIM, THEY SAID. HE had been twenty-three years in the army, the past seventeen in the cavalry out on the short grass. He was old and he knew he was old, but he was Schlonager. If he was sent to find a sod-house woman and three kids, he would find a sod-house woman and three kids. Not the woman and one kid. Or the woman and two kids. Or three kids without the woman. He would find the four of them. He would do that, or they would have to send out somebody else to find Schlonager. It was why they said of him in the regiment, that it took a tall horse to carry him.

Some say that Schlonager was a giant, six-and-one-half feet in height and weighing upward of 275 pounds. This would have drawn a grin even from Schlonager. And a groan from the very tallest horse. Size, as such, was not his secret. Nor was strength. True, a brawny recruit was always more easily persuaded to the right when his platoon sergeant could bend a cold horseshoe with the bare hand, or lift a loaded ammunition wagon on his back. Demonstrations of this caliber did impress. Yet Schlonager seldom had recourse to them, and his superiors, never. These latter knew their man and when there was trouble defiant to the facilities of the ordinary frontier garrison, they had an answer for it: "Send Schlonager."

Certain amenities were observed. The order was never given to Schlonager but to the handiest junior lieutenant who needed field experience. This unfortunate, the moment he had his column out of sight of the fort, invariably sang out the halt and inquired of his sergeant, "For God's sake, Schlonager, what do I do now?" In the present case of Lieutenant John Gilliam and the sod-house woman mission, Schlonager had nodded and in his impassive Teutonic manner replied as he always did: "Follow me."

Schlonager never said "sir" to junior officers. Nor, indeed, did he say it to field-grade officers below the rank of full colonel, in which case he said merely, "colonel." With general officers, particularly brigadiers and above who did not know him, he had been known to both say "sir" and to salute. But with working commands on tour west of Fort Lincoln the big German was disposed to save language. Understandably, since they had found it impractical to operate beyond the stockade without Schlonager, the commissions at Fort Pitchfork were of a common, charitable mind to play deaf to his abrupt responses.

Circumstances forever alter cases. Lieutenant Gilliam on this, his first official day in the field, was not playing deaf. He was playing host to a thick crust of blowflies which encased the canvas pack sheet covering his body. His orders had passed to the man who had been sent to carry them out in any event, Sergeant Honus Schlonager. For the troopers huddled behind the ridge this was all they had left to hang onto, and it was not enough. For the first time any of them could remember they knew doubt of the grizzled platoon leader.

The previous night they had slipped out of the stockade on a forced midnight march to prevent the ever-watchful enemy from guessing either the size or direction of their mission. All had gone well, as Schlonager had said it would. They had gotten cleanly away from the fort and into a good safe camp by daylight. Their resting place, the scrub timber of a small prairie creek, had relaxed all of them but Schlonager. He had ridden out in the gray dawn and scouted the way ahead five miles around. He had come back shaking his round head and growling to himself.

But a patrol of regular cavalry did not turn around and go back because the senior noncom objected to the "feel" of the coming day. When Lieutenant Gilliam brushed the sleep from his eyes and inquired if all were as it should be, Schlonager said yes, and that they could ride out as soon as the lieutenant was ready.

Thirty minutes later, they had come to the Cottonwood Rocks. It was a bad place, the fact being no secret reserved to Schlonager. Even though he had scouted it but one hour gone, he had Gilliam halt the patrol while he restudied the broken limestone ridges on either side of the military wagon road they were following eastward.

Finally, sighting a pair of sharp-tailed hawks

perched on the crest of the left-hand ridge, he indicated to Gilliam that the rocks were uninhabited, any detouring of them unnecessary. He had, he said, noted the female of the pair pivot her head to preen a wing feather, a certain sign that all was clear. Of course the birds would hold for the passage of the patrol which, being mounted and on the road where it belonged, would not frighten them. But the female would never be preening herself with any humans lying up in the rocks about her.

Since Schlonager was satisfied, Gilliam waved the "forward" without thought. His confidence in his sergeant was total. It had never been violated and it never was violated because the arrow which struck the young officer five minutes later entered the right eye socket and exploded out the base of the skull, carrying away with it one-quarter of his brain and all of his life so instantly there was no recording of even that "last flash" with which every man is reputed to die.

Schlonager fought the patrol out of the ambush with great skill. Three of the eight troopers were killed. With another sergeant, it may as well have been eight-in-eight, but the men would not see it that way. They rode on from that place with a new estimate of Schlonager's omnipotence. There was no disrespect in the altered view, only doubt. Yet that doubt gnawed on their nerves and worried at their imaginations without respite.

The prairie lay still and shimmering in the heat all

that morning. In the march across it only some antelope and a pair of buffalo wolves were seen. The antelope flagged and ran on sight, and the wolves circled far out around them, leading the men to suppose the animals had seen other humans that day. The talk of not going on after noon halt grew more open. Schlonager sensed the rebellion but ignored it. His corporal, Mario Scortini, angrily challenged it. How the devil, he demanded of the sullen troopers, could *any* white man foresee and guard against a device as cunning as those stuffed and mounted hawks? Had any of them ever heard of rigging dummy birds like that? With black horse-hair threads to make them move at the pull of the hidden Indian puppeteers? Well, hardly, by God! And yet they were blaming Schlonager for such a crazy thing. Now, damn it to hell, if a man couldn't have faith in a line sergeant who had survived seventeen years of such red trickery, he couldn't have faith in anything that wore stripes!

A Missouri recruit answering to the company tag of "Mudcat," spat a stream of tobacco juice at Scortini's boot tips. "I had a friend," he drawled, "who was a squad corporal with the Seventh Cavalry. This feller had a passel of faith in his sergeant, yes sir. He even had the same general blessing of confidence in his regimental commander. Some of you boys might remember that officer," he concluded acidly. "Custer, I think his name was."

The analogy was valid and recent. So was the geography. Where they were presently slowing their mounts for the noon-halt coffee ration, they were within two rides of the Little Big Horn. On the calendar it was something just over a year since Yellow Hair and his 226 men had died on that brown hill above the clear shallows of the "Greasy Grass."

The halt was made and broken in a continuing silence. When Schlonager said "mount up," they stood and eyed him to the man. He had already started for his own horse when he realized they were not moving. He turned around, looking at them as though they had taken leave of their senses. "Corporal," he said quietly, "repeat the order."

Scortini did so.

The men looked at one another. They would not look at Schlonager. But they didn't move to get on their horses. Schlonager walked past Scortini. "Which one of you," he said to the men, "is the new sergeant?"

There was one, he knew. There was always one in every company. It took a little trouble to smoke him out, usually, but with this bunch, separating the agitator was apt to prove a nice field problem. They were all volunteers, a fact which guaranteed nothing except the high-risk nature of their mission. Three of them were old regulars, two were first-hitchers. None of them were young men. None of them would have been picked by Schlonager for this work.

"Harry—?" said Schlonager quietly.

"Not me, Sergeant." The thin, balding trooper spoke with a broad English accent. "As you know, I'm the soul of honor."

Schlonager nodded with the least lift of an eyebrow, singled out the next man. "Squint—?"

He had been a cowboy most probably, a trail driver, say. He was tall, bowlegged, dry-humored; a droll but not simple Galahad of the southern plains, whose only steady work had been as a stage robber on the old Smoky Hill line of the Overland Mail Company. He had taken his nickname from his past and from the attendant habit of peering constantly behind him to detect the overdue dust of the El Paso or Salina posses. Schlonager figured he would shoot his man down with the same twinkle in the friendly gray eye with which he would buy him a drink.

"No sir," said Squint. "I ain't bucking for no promotions."

"Pulaski—?"

The Pole was from the eastern coal mines. The story that had transferred with him from outfit to outfit the past eleven years was that he had killed his wife. Why, or how, was never mentioned. He was simply "the wife killer." Schlonager suspected he was more than that, but the broad blond man with the thick yellow hair had never spoken to clear himself of the name. He had only moved on and on through the regiments of the frontier, hoping, it seemed, to lose his past along the way.

"No," answered Pulaski blankly and after long staring at the ground. "I want nothing."

Schlonager moved his eyes to Ira Shank, ex-Redleg Kansas Jayhawker and John Brown Abolitionist, one

19

of the two "new" men on the patrol. "Shank—?" he said.

The Kansan shook his head. He was a short, wide-shouldered man, with a brown beard and piercing blue eyes. He had the look of the fanatic to him, Schlonager thought, but he had been a model soldier since his arrival on post from Fort Riley. "If I was after rank, Sergeant," he told his questioner, "it wouldn't be yours. No offense, of course."

"Of course," said Schlonager expressionlessly, moving on to the last man. "Clevenger—?"

This was the one called Mudcat, the Missourian who made no secret of his Confederate guerrilla past with the Clay County cavalry of Bloody Bill Anderson and Barney Poole. He was a salmon-jawed, mean-eyed man, with a shriveled left arm from the sack of Lawrence, and a certain understanding that the South had never surrendered. Schlonager knew less of him than of any of them, except to know that he would bear the most watching of them all. "*Clevenger?*" he repeated.

Mudcat's pale eyes glared. The lean muscles about his mouth twitched. "You go to hell," he said.

Schlonager hit him with his left hand in the pit of the stomach and, as he doubled forward, he hit him again, with his right hand, behind the ear. He went to his knees, half conscious but unable to rise. "Help him on his horse," said Schlonager to the others, and turned for his own mount. This time he did not look back and the men did not hesitate. They got Clevenger in his saddle and found their own quickly. The Englishman, unbidden, took the lead rope of the pack string carrying the bodies of Lieutenant Gilliam and their dead comrades. The others went ahead of him, bunching their mounts behind Schlonager and Scortini. "Single file!" snapped the latter, seeing them crowd in. "One-mount intervals!" The men obeyed, knowing the reason. Single file it was hard to talk without being overheard. Without talking, concerted action was unlikely. But something had been decided by the halt, nonetheless. It was clear in Scortini's sharp command to space out. The corporal was staying with Schlonager.

The afternoon wore away in a hell of heat and dryness. Sundown came on and with it they came to the last rise in the prairie before the drop-off into the valley of the Big Horn River. Schlonager waved the halt behind a sheltering outcrop of stone and stunted pine. He and Scortini dismounted and climbed the rocky reef. At the top, Schlonager uncased his field glasses, began studying the red-hazed miles below them. His corporal crouched beside him, watching not the sunset heat waves of the valley, ahead, but the parched and sullen faces of the troopers, behind.

"See anything?" he asked Schlonager.

"Not yet."

The stillness resettled itself.

"Honus," said Scortini, "let's turn back; I'm getting jumpy."

"You're a poor liar," said Schlonager, without

21

taking down the glasses. "You could sleep in a sack of snakes without twitching."

Scortini grinned. He was a murderous-looking little man, as dark and restless as a Chacma baboon. He was as moral, too. In the ordinary sense he very likely did not understand the meaning of physical fear. Yet he was feeling something.

"Well," he grudged, "maybe I'm hungry. It hits you in the same place, in the guts."

"Never mind the guts," said Schlonager, handing him the glasses. "You see anything?"

Scortini took the glasses and focused them. "No," he answered, after a long minute.

"Down there left of that creek coming in on this side; the one with the good timber along it," said Schlonager. "Screw down tight on that pothole meadow saucered in by that rim of base rock."

"By God!" muttered the corporal. "I never would have spotted it. That damn sodbuster hid it pretty good."

"Yeah, see anything else?"

"You mean Indians? No. Far as I can make out from here there ain't a Sioux in Wyoming Territory south of Sheridan."

Schlonager grunted softly. "Except the dozen that ambushed us this morning, eh?" he said.

"Oh, hell!" objected the little man, returning the glasses. "That wasn't your fault, Honus. You know that."

"Maybe," said the other. He jerked his head

slightly, indicating the men behind them. "They don't know it, though."

Scortini looked down at the men. They were staring upward, watching Schlonager. "I can feel their eyes in my back," the latter said. "We've got more than Indians to fight, I'm thinking." Scortini nodded. "Yeah," he said. Both men looked back to the valley. "Mario," said the big sergeant, "did you see any life around that soddie?" Scortini shook his head. "Not a flicker," he said. "Did you?" Schlonager made no motion either of agreement or denial. In his deliberate way, he refocused the glasses. Slowly, he moved them, first north and south along the river, then easterly, beyond it, toward the Tensleep country and Fort McKinney. Lastly, he came down and steadied on the widow woman's place. The furnace heat of day's end clutched smotheringly at the silent buildings and the empty meadow surrounding them. If there were life in that sun-baked clearing, Schlonager could not see it; and Schlonager saw very well. He lowered the glasses. "We'll go on, anyway," he said. "You never know."

Scortini knew better; he knew what Schlonager thought. But all he said was, "Sure, I'll tell the boys."

"Tell them," said Schlonager, "to keep close."

The corporal scrambled down the rocky slope. "Sergeant says to keep close," he told the waiting men.

"You mean we're going on, Wop?"

They called him that, all of them, except Schlonager. He had never resented it, particularly, until Clevenger came along with his Southerner's superior talent for making a dirty word of it. He now eyed the lantern-jawed guerrilla carefully. Resentment or not, he wanted no part of Mudcat Clevenger. "Don't know," he replied to the question. "Sergeant only said to keep close."

"Like hell he did," rasped the other. "I seen him motion to you like as we would go on. Don't give me none of them innocent stares, you hear?"

"For Pete's sake," pleaded Scortini, low-voiced, "shut up! He's watching us."

"I don't care a bushel of bull chips what the hell he's doing!" snarled the Southerner. "He ain't no officer and I ain't a'follering him another goddam step. He's a'ready got the lieutenant and three others of us kilt, and he's a'trying to do the same for the rest of us, so's we cain't testify agin him when we get back. Well, by God, here's one boy he ain't going to dump across no horse. Now, you tell him that, monkey-grinder!"

"*Madre!*" groaned Scortini, glancing upward, "I won't need to—he *heard* you."

The men moved wordlessly away from Clevenger. After a moment's hesitation, Scortini joined them. Left alone, the rebel lifted his lip like a cornered coyote but he did not whimper nor attempt to run. In the increasing quiet, the clinking roll of small stones dislodged by Schlonager's descent of the rise was strangely loud.

24

The old sergeant moved stiffly. He had now ridden twenty hours without sleep. Darkness and danger crowded close. It was obvious that he could not delay in this place, yet he did not seem to hurry. Clevenger began to worry. He did not know the big German. He thought that he was handicapped in this, that the others were in possession of information he was not, that all of them, not just the big dumb sergeant, were against him. He felt what all men feel when their fellows cast them out. This was what concerned him, not Schlonager.

Schlonager stopped in front of him. He removed his shirt, folded it according to regulations, placed it carefully upon a clean patch of the hard ground. He unhooked belt and holster, laid them upon the shirt. Only then did he nod to the other man. Clevenger's light eyes narrowed the least bit. He shucked off his shirt, pulled belt and holster loose, kicked both articles away from him as he dropped them. When he was ready, he said no more than Schlonager, merely returned the other's opening nod. Behind him, the men drew in silently—the pack gathering instinctively, the response as old as the dim origins of the race. A formless sound rumbled among them. They were watching Schlonager. They knew what was coming.

2

IT WAS THE WOLF AGAINST THE BEAR. THE CHALLENGER against the aging champion. The swift against the staunch.

Clevenger hurt Schlonager. He kneed him, gouged him, kicked, clawed, elbowed, bit and fouled in every way known to the wicked and unfair. He tried to put his spurs into his kidneys and, one time, struck at his eyes with a jagged sliver of rock which came beneath his groping hand. He split one ear with his teeth, threw dust to blind, tripped, feigned injury, leaped full on when Schlonager fell, attempted with every movement and moment to impair the other man.

Schlonager fought another fight. He, too, meant to hurt. But he did not mean to maim. It was his intention to beat Thurman Clevenger senseless and toward that end he moved as relentlessly as age and stiffness and honor would allow him.

When the Southerner went down for the eighth time in half that many minutes, he knew he was beaten, and Schlonager knew he had him beaten. But Clevenger was the breed of dog who would not quit, conscious. When he came, this time, unsteadily to his feet, he came with a drawn knife in his right hand. The tense soldiers caught the flash of the blade in the late sun and leaped to disarm him, but Schlonager hoarsely roared for them to stand back, to let their comrade come on as he would. The troopers from long habit of obedience to Honus Schlonager hesitated and fell back. The gray-haired sergeant moved in on Clevenger, his eyes never leaving the knife in the latter's right hand. The knife and the knife hand were all that counted now. All else was blurred. He would have to take the gleaming steel in one way, or the other. Either he took it by his own hand, or he took it in his own guts, and there was no other choice. In the final half second, Clevenger, knowing as well as Schlonager where life and death lay, played his treacherous blade for what it might be worth. With a motion quick as the flickering of an adder's tongue, he moved the knife from his good right to his withered left hand, the token of his service on the day that Lawrence, Kansas, burned in the name of sweet slavery, the hand that no man there had imagined was of a strength or skill to hold and wield any weapon, unsupported, and with the left hand he struck the blade in a whistling slash toward the undefended groin of his enemy.

What saved Schlonager was a fistfighter's natural move to turn with the coming blow. He did not get clear of the knife but his lowered right elbow caught the force of the blade, turning it aside. It went into his hip, grounded on the bone, twisted and flew out of Clevenger's hand. Schlonager brought his knee up under the unguarded chin of his opponent. The force of the lift sent the Southerner flying backward, staggering off balance. His heel caught on a small stone, and he fell back, landing heavily. Before he could move, Schlonager was over him and drove his boot into the side of his head with the short, final, crushing stomp that he would use to stun a run-over cur, or an injured wild animal. Clevenger's whole body arched upward in a spinal bow, then collapsed and lay sprawled and oddly small and crumpled in the buffalo grass.

After what seemed a long time, Scortini moved out and knelt by his side. He looked into his eyes by lifting the swollen lids. The balls were rolled up and locked. He raised the slack head, turning it to see if the neck were broken. It did not seem to be. Scortini stood up.

"Well, he's not dead," he announced.

"I'm glad he isn't," said Schlonager simply. "Put him across his horse."

Scortini hesitated, eyeing the bodies of the lieutenant and the three troopers. "You mean like those?" he asked uneasily.

"Sure," said Schlonager. "It'll give him something to think about when he wakes up."

The corporal nodded and turned away. "If he ever does," he muttered to himself.

They draped Clevenger over his mount's saddle, not knowing, really, if he were yet alive, or not.

"Damn," growled Pulaski, in one of his rare statements. "Now we got another load of blowfly bait. It ain't what we need. Damn to hell."

Squint Hibbard, the philosophic highwayman, patted the Pole's thick shoulder. "Never you mind,

Bohunkie," he soothed. "At least he won't lack for friends along the way. Just look at them bodies, yonder. Why, it's enough to start up your very own morchuary."

The squat coal miner peered unblinkingly at the dead lieutenant and the three soldiers. The bodies of the troopers had no canvas covers, like that of the officer, to protect their swollen faces. The blowflies clotted in black and bottle-green windrows about the eyes, mouths, nostrils of the corpses seeking for the moisture of the mucous membranes long since dehydrated. Pulaski crossed himself. Squint nodded, no longer grinning.

"That's a good idea," he said. "Make one of them for me, Bohunkie."

The Pole shook his head.

"You got to make your own," he said, and went for his horse.

3

DESCENDING THE BLUFF TO THE LOWER PRAIRIE AND going over it toward the sod-house woman's place, the patrol moved with no sound other than that of an occasional squeak of leather or clink of spur chain. The tired horses were kept at the trot. They were losing daylight and Schlonager did not care to come in on those silent buildings at dusk. While he led his survivors through that final stifling half hour of their ill-fated march, his mind reached back to the mis-

29

sion's beginning, conscientiously reworking the entire trail to the bluffs of the Big Horn.

The instructions given Lieutenant Gilliam had been meager—go out into Greybull Basin somewhere between the Bittersweet and Gooseberry Creek crossings of the Big Horn and look for the Shuffman woman and her three children. Schlonager could still hear Captain Hobart's closing words, the words spoken to Gilliam but intended for Schlonager: "Beat the Sioux to them, Lieutenant; and don't come back without them." Those were words that would never appear on the order-of-record. They wouldn't look good in Washington, or even Fort Lincoln. Not after the Custer thing. But Hobart was an officer up through the ranks. One of the rare ones on the frontier without the West Point ring. He didn't know Uncle Billy Sherman, or Little Phil Sheridan, or Ranald Mackenzie, George Crook, O. O. Howard, or any of the other front-page Indian experts in the War Department. All he knew were the *Cavalry Regulations, Cavalry Close Order Drill, Field Manual of Small Arms* and old Nate Forrest's Civil War advice to all good horse soldiers, "Get there fustest with the mostest."

Thinking of his C. O.'s aggressive attitude, Schlonager shook his head. Blunt orders and bluff confidence were not enough. A man had to know *something,* and in this case the information upon which the mission was based had been even more cryptic than Hobart's "go get 'em" order.

The homesteader had been found scalped and left for dead on the military wagon road which ran from Fort McKinney west to Fort Pitchfork. The courier who found him had been bound for Pitchfork from McKinney. The place was between Tensleep and the Big Horn, east of the river, and the man had said seven words, accompanied by a last pointing of his hand to the west, before dying in the trooper's arms. The words had been, "Shuffman . . . Sioux . . . wife . . . kids . . . three . . . Gooseberry . . . Bittersweet." It was this grim set of directions which Hobart had handed on to Honus Schlonager via John Gilliam, the dead lieutenant.

Again, the big sergeant's round head wagged fretfully.

"It's crazy," he said softly. "Absolutely pure daft . . ."

The McKinney courier said they did not know Shuffman on his post. None of the personnel at Pitchfork had heard of him, either. That is, not for the record. Oh, there had been a rumor months earlier that some tomfool of a sod-house squatter had sneaked into the Tensleep or Greybull basins. Word of it had come from a reservation Sioux who had the report, in turn, from a wild cousin who suggested he tell the Pony Soldiers about it, so that they could move the man and his family out and save everyone the bad feeling of another Indian raid. No effort had been made to check out the information other than the standard army procedure in such cases: each of the involved posts, Pitchfork and McKinney, requesting

31

the other to take care of the matter and then both conveniently forgetting all about it. For the third time Schlonager growled and shook his gray head. *The stupid blind fools,* he thought.

The Greybull and Tensleep country had been closed to new settlement since the massacre of the Seventh Cavalry fourteen months before. The army had done its *official* best to dissuade the foolhardy from tarrying where roving packs of bandit Sioux and Cheyenne still constituted a clear and present danger. But in the actual field sense it had done little to police the matter. Not few brave or avaricious whites managed to evade the law and its military minions, and settle in upon these forbidden lands.

One of these latter had been the man Shuffman.

He had died for his courage, or his greed, it was true. It might be argued that this balanced his account. Schlonager could not agree. Whatever Shuffman had settled by dying, his estate was still open and he, Schlonager, had inherited the chanceful assignment of closing it. No experienced sergeant of regular cavalry could fail to appreciate the opportunity.

It was that time in Wyoming-Montana Indian history between the Crook-Custer-Gibbon-Terry smash at the Sioux on the Rosebud and the Little Big Horn, and the wiping out of the Dull Knife Cheyenne by Captain Wessels and the killer cavalry from Fort Robinson, Nebraska. Schlonager well comprehended this fact, and its immediate implications for him and his men were scarcely lost upon him. The main numbers of the hostile Sioux had fled to Canada with Gall and Sitting Bull after the Little Big Horn. The Cheyenne had been trapped and transported to Oklahoma, there to be penned like slaughter cattle on the hot, malarial plain near Fort Reno. But outlaw bands of both tribes still prowled the northern prairies in search of white stragglers. Their hunting method was impossible to defense. They would drift down from the rough lands of the Missouri's headwaters, strike on the run and in widely separated places, be gone back up into the trackless wilderness of the Judith Basin and the Bear Paws before the frustrated military could so much as agree to go after them. In the brief time since Custer's debacle, forty-one white killings had been reported in north central Wyoming alone. Of these, a few were Oregon and California-bound emigrants cut off from their parties by accident or sickness. But most, such as the Shuffmans, were of that irrational, wrongheaded strain which would settle where God, Nature, natural intelligence and the United States Army maintained they should not. These unwanted "stayers" in the Indian Domain were the ones the hostiles tracked down with a particular vengeance reserved entirely to their ignorant ranks. Schlonager knew this, the army knew it, the territorial government knew it: it was not the members of the military, not the civilian travelers through their ancestral hunting preserves whom the Indians hated so cordially; it was the pig-stubborn, selfish and irresponsible men and women who insisted upon remaining where they were warned not to remain, who brought down upon such patrols as that of Sergeant Honus Schlonager's all the grief, ugliness and despair that made up the bitter record of the United States Cavalry on the frontier.

All of this Schlonager understood poignantly, all of it yet toiled within his weary mind, as his lathered roan stumbled through the sunset dust toward the dark trees and red-stained rocks marking the confluence of Gooseberry Creek with the Big Horn River.

Perhaps it was this very preoccupation with the whole of his situation that distracted him momentarily from its detail. Again, it may have been a pseudo-confidence imparted by the serene view, taken through the field glasses from the bluff, of the settler's shanty and its outlying stock shed. It could have been, too, no more than physical exhaustion from the long ride, without sleep, and in such intense heat. As well, it may have been that all of them upon the patrol were at fault; that every man there was too turned inward in his doubting and hatred and suspicion and fear of his comrades, to be on normal guard against the alien stillness that surrounded them all. The reason might be argued endlessly; the result could not.

When they rode through the saucer-rim of rock enclosing the Shuffman meadow, there were no more than five minutes of shooting light remaining, and those five would be for close shooting only. The advance columns of the night were already marching too far out from the flanking hills to permit of anything like aimed fire at a distance greater than thirty or forty feet. Unquestionably, this fact, too, contributed to the momentary lulling of nerves; this, and the unexpected surprise of seeing a light shining from the cabin window.

"By God," said Scortini, spitting through the dust that caked his monkey's grimace, "we've made it in time!"

Schlonager straightened. Taken in its context of the peaceful meadow, singing creek water, welcoming lamplight and seeming safe ending to their search for the Shuffman family, the remark was warranted. But Schlonager was a conservative man. "Maybe," he said. "We'll just pull on past that clump of bull pine and hail the house. You never can tell."

"*Maria!*" burst out the volatile Latin, "you wouldn't recognize your own mother unless she brought along your birth certificate to prove who she was. I'd sure hate to owe you money!"

"I'd hate to have you," shrugged Schlonager, not unaffectionately. "You'd cut off your kid sister's nubbins for a nickel."

Scortini grinned darkly. "If I couldn't first sell her virtue for a dime," he admitted, "yes. But you can't mix blood with business ordinarily. It don't pay. 'Slit the throat and take the purse, but never say hello,' that's the motto of my tribe. You might be cutting up a friend, or a first cousin. Like you say, you never can tell."

"You should have been a Sioux," scowled Schlonager.

"Never!" protested the other. "They ain't in it with us Sicilians!"

Schlonager nodded, conceding the point. "Column-twos, men," he said softly to the troopers behind them. "Let's look like cavalry coming in."

They went forward, skirting the stand of pine. Rounding its far side, Schlonager came to an unbidden halt. Scortini said, "*Jeezzz—!*" long and sibilantly between his teeth, and brought his own mount to the dead stand. Behind them the four troopers and the five loaded packhorses piled up, the animals pricking their ears and flaring their nostrils to the overwhelming rank scent of enemy horseflesh that came to them from in front.

After a straining silence upon both sides, Schlonager put up his hand, palm out, and said hopefully, "*Hau, kola, tahunsa*—greetings, we come as friends, as cousins"; but he well knew that it was a lame lie and that the Sioux would not "uncover their ears" to it. To his own side he made a more useful suggestion out of the corner of his mouth— "don't nobody move a muscle"—and then sat waiting for the ax to fall. The leader of the hostiles identified himself by moving his pony a length out in front of his companions. He was a young man and extremely handsome, with a deep, melodious voice that now fell upon the startled ears of the Pitchfork patrol in measured accents of perfectly clear, if guttural and abridged, English. "Good joke," he said to Schlonager. "White man makes a good joke. But I don't laugh."

"Neither does the white man," vowed Schlonager soberly. He ran his eyes around the circle of warriors flanking the young chief. "You have picked up more men since you tried my soldiers this morning. Now we'll have a better fight."

The Sioux shook his head.

"No fight," he said, "slaughter. Look behind."

Schlonager, careful not to hurry, did so. More mounted Sioux were drifting out of the pines to close the circle of the surround. It was all so simple and peaceful and nicely done that it deceived the mind. Another sergeant than Honus Schlonager would have made some fatal miscalculations about now. The tone and manner of the young Indian were restrained. His English meant that he had been on the reservation— no doubt Pine Ridge—a long time; in his few words he had managed to convey an impression that he was a reasonable and even kindly fellow. He seemed, too, to be in control of his followers, something by no means common with Indian war parties. The entire band did not act as though they meant anything but to palaver with an idea of bluffing the soldiers out of some tobacco and possibly their blanket rolls and canteens, items of real and constant value to nomad horsemen. Yet these were the same Indians who had, twelve hours earlier, laid up in a bow-and-arrow ambush of the deadliest type and intent, killing four men and meaning to kill eleven.

Schlonager said as quietly as he could, to Scortini,

"How many do you make all together?"

"Thirty," answered the corporal. "How about you?"

"Less. Maybe two dozen. We'll fight."

"Why?" asked the Sioux leader.

As low as the white men had held their voices, his keen hearing had picked up the words. Schlonager tensed.

"Why not?" he said.

"We don't want to kill you," shrugged the young Indian.

"Sure," said Schlonager bitingly. "That's why you put those stuffed hawks in the Cottonwood Rocks this morning."

"Not true. We only wanted your guns, bridles, saddles, all your things that we can use. It's the same tonight. Give us the things and go. The times are hard. My people want for many needs. We can't trade any more. We fear to go near the posts. My men were afraid to talk to you this morning; that's why we shot you instead. Now it's nearly dark. We can't shoot each other so well. They don't think you will shoot. I told them you would not. I took this chance. Now what do you say, Schlonager?"

The old sergeant was startled by the use of his name. He peered hard at the young Sioux. "You know me?" he asked doubtfully. "How is that?"

The Indian lifted his naked shoulders. "Most easy," he replied. "You big like grizzly bear, you have hair tipped with silver gray like his, you fight like him. Who else you be?"

38

"Yeah," subsided Scortini, "I guess."

The white soldiers fell silent. Across from them, the Indians had been holding a consultation of their own, accounting for the opportunity to talk granted Schlonager and his subordinate. Now the red conference was also finished. Crow Mane turned from it back to the sergeant.

"We have decided," he said. "We were thinking if to kill you or let you go. Ordinarily, it would have been small matter. But we have already killed five of you, as can easily be counted by the bodies over there." He pointed to the standing packhorses and their motionless burdens. "It was good you brought them along to bury in a proper way, Schlonager. If the bodies had not been here—" he shrugged and smiled, and Schlonager shivered. He knew what the Sioux meant. If the bodies had not been there for him to point out to his comrades, the war party would never have agreed to spare the rest of the patrol. "Thank you, Crow Mane," he said. "You were always wise."

"My friends don't agree, but I have convinced them that to scatter more blood for the soldiers from the big fort to follow, would be foolish."

He meant Fort McKinney, and Schlonager nodded. "Good thinking. Now what will we do?"

"You will leave everything you have with you. Pile it all on the ground. Right here." He pointed to a spot in front of his pony. "Then you will walk away toward your fort and don't turn back to look at us. You can even take the bodies of your friends, except

41

for their hair. We took that in honest fight this morning, and my men want to have it and I have said yes to them. That's all."

Schlonager's blunt jaw squared itself. Scortini's Latin heart sank. The four soldiers behind them licked cracked and spittle-glazed lips and swallowed tightly. Every eye in the huddled troop went to the packhorses, singling out the fifth body. *Clevenger!* They had all forgotten Clevenger hanging there as limply and as still as Gilliam and the others. But *was* he as were they? Could they sit there and agree to leave him, not knowing? The questions went, with the anxious glances, back to Honus Schlonager.

The big German only nodded.

"If you touch those bodies," he told Crow Mane, "the shooting will begin. Plenty squaws will howl when you get home. You know me; you decide."

This was not a bluff, Crow Mane was certain. He did, indeed, know this man. Schlonager. But the position was awkward. Another council with his braves might not end so favorably for all. Yet Schlonager, too, would shoot when he said he would. *He-hau!* It was not always so easy to be a chief.

"And if we leave the hair?" he temporized. There was no reaction from his braves because none of them understood English well enough to keep up with a quick talk such as this one, and the sergeant was keeping his voice down and his face straight. But the danger was there and both he and Schlonager were aware of it.

"Take our horses, guns, whatever you want," the latter replied carefully. "But just take them and get out. You do it that way, and it will be remembered in your favor. Otherwise—" He shrugged, leaving it there.

The young Sioux studied him.

"You're a good man, Schlonager," he admitted at last and, Scortini thought, a little sadly. "I think we do that what you say. We better take the things and go home." He turned to his warriors. "*Hopo!*" he barked in Sioux. "Take their guns and be careful but quick."

It was when he said that, when three of his followers swung down from their ponies to begin lifting from the cavalry scabbards the short 7-shot Spencer carbines prized above all the weapons, save the Winchester, by the hostiles of the North Plains, that it happened. There was no warning for either side. One moment it was a quiet and orderly, if tense, disarming of captured troops. The next instant it was an abattoir. Mudcat Clevenger, recovering consciousness in that critical pause and seeing the situation going forward between his comrades and the Oglala war party, unsheathed his own Spencer. None of the Sioux were watching the "dead men's horses," and none of the white soldiers either. The silent rifleman began firing with deadly, point-blank precision into the Indian riders flanking Crow Mane. The first to fall, clutching his breast and crying out with the low moan of a stricken animal, was the young chief himself.

4

IT WAS BLACK DARK, THE INDIANS WERE GONE. TWO MEN were posted at the stock shed: Ira Shank and Mudcat Clevenger. Two more stood guard at the far corner of the cabin commanding the clearing in the opposite direction: Harry Albion and Squint Hibbard. The Pole, Pulaski, who had some post hospital experience, was in the cabin with Scortini, Schlonager and the wounded Crow Mane. The stillness, over all the clearing, was as intense as the August heat which seemed to have increased, not abated, with the coming of night.

"What do you think?" said Schlonager to the Pole.

"It's hot," said the latter. "If it wasn't so damned hot."

"We could take him outside. Would that help?"

"Maybe. I don't know."

"Well, thanks, Pulaski. You cleaned him up good."

"Yes, that much I could do."

They sat silently, crouching over the Indian youth, having done what they could, and knowing it.

"*Santa!*" mumbled Scortini, "let's take him outside. I can't stand it in here. I never felt it so hot."

Schlonager nodded, standing up.

"It's a funny thing," he said. "A man gets hurt and we right away want to get him inside, or under shelter. Why? It doesn't help. Sometimes it harms, maybe."

"Hell," shrugged Scortini, "it's instinct. You get hit, you do the same thing—drag yourself to cover."

"Yes, but why?"

"Why? Christ, I don't know why. Probably so we won't get hit again."

"Sure, but that's in a continuing fight. This is a different thing. Here there's no danger right now."

"Look, Honus." Scortini palmed his hands defensively. "It's hot. We got the lieutenant and three soldiers dead. We got this Indian kid dying. We got his friends out there in the dark waiting for the sun and good shooting light to finish us off. We got five men left who want to desert or drill us in the back first chance they get. We got an eighteen-hour ride back to the fort. We got horses that are already rode down to their hocks. We got—well, Jesus, Honus, we got trouble. Let's talk about *that*."

The ponderous sergeant stood another moment, thinking.

"No," he finally said, "let's not talk about what we got; let's talk about what we haven't got."

"You mean like cold beer, clean bed sheets, a bosomy brunette?"

"No. I mean like that prairie woman and her three kids."

Scortini winced. "My God," he said, "I'd forgotten the poor things; that'll show you how hot it is."

"I don't think those Sioux got to them," said Schlonager. "Maybe some others, but not this bunch. I wish we knew."

Scortini did not answer him, nor did Pulaski, but he was answered. He felt the touch of the hesitant red hand on his leg, and looked down. Crow Mane was conscious, staring up at him. "We don't see the woman when we come here," he told Schlonager. "No little ones either. Nothing here."

Schlonager knelt swiftly. He took the Indian boy's hand in his own huge paw, patting it gently. "How do you feel?" he asked. "Did you hear us talking about you just now?"

What may have been an Oglala smile flickered over the boy's handsome face. "I don't have to hear you, Schlonager," he murmured. "I can hear the bullet. It is talking to me—listen to it." He held up a slim finger and all three white men bent forward in unthinking unison. The sound of the breath laboring in his torn lungs was an ugly, accusing thing. The white soldiers exchanged silent, guilty looks.

"You hear it?" asked Crow Mane. "What does anyone think it is saying to me?"

Schlonager shook his head, stubbornly refusing the idea. But Pulaski crossed himself and Scortini, when he thought he was unobserved, did the same. The stillness became unbearable. Schlonager stood up.

"If it was me," he said, looking down, "I would like it to be outside. What do you say, Little Brother?"

The Indian youth nodded, eyes closed now.

"You know my heart, Schlonager," he said. "I am Oglala. This is no place for a proud man to wait for Yunke Lo. I thank you, *tahunsa*. You good friend. Long time I know this about you."

Schlonager stared down at him a moment, broad face working, big hands knotting and unknotting.

46

"Long time you know nothing," he said at last, and with bitter softness, stooped and lifted him in his great arms, lightly as a child, and carried him out of the noxious sod house into the clean Wyoming night.

5

SCHLONAGER WENT QUIETLY THROUGH THE DUST OF THE clearing toward the stock shed. It was about 10:00 P.M. now and he came only to check his guards in the shed and to be sure they were standing their watch as ordered; two hours off, two hours on, through the night. Clevenger's had been the first two hours, so he expected to find and talk to the other man, Ira Shank. He was surprised, then, upon nearing the small log-and-sod structure, to hear two voices. Alerted by the instincts of well-nigh a quarter century of soldiering, he came even more carefully the last few feet of the way, pausing in the shadows of the shed to hear what it might be that kept two weary troopers awake after twenty hours in the saddle.

Shank had a dry voice, the kind that carries and cuts. He was cutting with it now.

"Thirteen years," he was saying, "thirteen years, six months, seven days. Do you remember it, Clevenger?"

If Mudcat Clevenger did remember it, he was not ready to admit the fact. "I don't know what the hell I'm supposed to remember," he said, "but I'm listening. Talking to anybody is better than sitting here listening to them damned Sioux making no noise at all."

"Thirteen years," repeated Shank, "and you haven't changed a bit—you're still a murdering cold-blooded son of a sick dog."

"Sweet Murphy!" said the other man, "I wisht you would come out with it. You been beating around about me and them thirteen years ever since supper. Long as I cain't sleep and I got to listen, I wisht you'd break it open."

"No you don't," said Shank, "because after I break it open, I'm going to kill you."

"Shank, you're crazy. What the hell you mean, you're going to kill me? The heat must of got you out there today. You're sun-strick, mister; you're sick."

"No," said Shank, "at least not from the sun, or from the Sioux, like you must be."

"Sick from the Sioux? Me? What you getting at, Shank? You really are daft, ain't you?"

"You know well what I mean about the Sioux," said Ira Shank. "You shot down that young chief in cold blood. I know you, Clevenger, I know you from a long time. You were lying to Sergeant Schlonager this evening when you told him how it was. It couldn't have been that innocent, sensible way. Not with you. Not with your kind, Clevenger. You don't kill for any cause except your own wicked lust, your own stupid hatred and meanness."

Clevenger slewed around on his haunches, facing him in the blind darkness.

"You do talk a whole lot, mister," he said carefully. "Where at you know me from? How come you saying

48

you know me from a long time? I don't know you, Shank. I never seen you in my life before you transferred out to Pitchfork."

"We were talking about that young chief," said Ira Shank. "The one you shot in cold blood, and told Schlonager you thought was meaning to kill him and the rest of us. Admit it, Clevenger. You came to in plenty of time to know the Indians weren't going to harm us. You just waited over there in the cover of those horses with our dead on them. You let it go just so long, until you had that Sioux boy in your sights and could bring him down like a stalked sheep. Am I right, Clevenger? I would like to have your testimony on the record before I execute my own judgment upon you. Even a murdering dog deserves his day in court."

"What the hell you saying? You talk like you was the Circuit Judge and had me by the heels on a murder warrant for certain sure. What you want of me?"

"I think you knew exactly what you were doing and what the Indians and Sergeant Schlonager were doing when you drew down on that Oglala boy. You heard that he and Schlonager knew one another, and you heard him and Schlonager agree to part friendly, with the Indians taking our stuff and leaving us unharmed. You lied to Schlonager when you told him you had just come to and thought the Indians were about to attack us and shoot us down in cold blood."

"What you mean, Shank? What you trying to say?"

"That you tried," replied Ira Shank slowly, "to kill the young Sioux exactly, and with the same brute cunning and cruelty and madness, as you tried to kill those poor defenseless farm and town folk in Belle Prairie."

"*Belle Prairie—?*"

Mudcat said it hesitantly and underbreath, as a man will when he recalls the sound but not the sense of a name.

"*Kansas,*" amplified Shank sibilantly.

"Lord God," muttered the Southerner after a long pause, "so that's what was thirteen years ago!"

"Plus six months and seven days," said Ira Shank.

Schlonager, waiting by the shed wall, tensed. He could see the silhouettes of his two soldiers where they sat in the open face of the shed, watching out across the clearing toward the river. He felt the imminence of the move by one, or both of them, to go at the other. But he still did not make his own move to interfere. He felt that he had not heard all that was to be said here, before the men broke, and so he waited, ready to leap at them but not knowing for what reason, or at what time, or in support of which of them, he would make that leap.

"That was a bad day," said Mudcat Clevenger. "The last raid our outfit made into Kansas. Was your folks mixed inter it, Shank? I don't remember Belle Prairie as well as a man ought, I suppose. I was fair drunk likely. But I hearn the name somewheres before and I reckon you're right that I was there and done my share."

50

"I'm right," said Shank, "and so are you. You were there and my folks were mixed into it and you did your share."

"Well, war ain't nice," replied Mudcat, not unreasonably. "Sometimes it gets fair ugly."

"Yes," said Shank, "especially when you're drunk and killing nigger lovers in free-state Kansas."

"My God," said Mudcat, "you got a wicked-long memory."

"And accurate, Clevenger. Those were your exact words when I pleaded with you not to shoot my two brothers and old Uncle Thurman that afternoon in Belle Prairie."

Again, Schlonager felt he should move in, and felt he should not move in, and so stood listening.

"Was those your brothers?" asked Mudcat. "Them two towheaded kids with that rheumatized old nigger down by the river? The ones what shot at me with that damned scatter-gun when I yelled at them to halt?"

"Those were my brothers. Ben was fourteen, Cletus, eleven."

"I didn't aim to hit them," said Mudcat. "I meant to get the old nigger."

"Sure," said Shank, "that's why you emptied your carbine. Seven shots to kill one poor old crippled colored man at forty feet."

"The light was bad, damn it; I ain't no kid killer."

"It was four o'clock in the afternoon, and no clouds."

"It was dark down in that river brush where they

was trying to sneak that old darkie into that boat and get him acrost and on the other side. And they was big kids. I thought they was men. Besides, I was on sentry duty."

"Yes," said Shank, "and drunk."

The stillness closed in so thickly then that Schlonager was convinced they must hear his compressed breathing, but they did not.

"Shank," said Mudcat Clevenger at last, "I am sorry abouten them boys. I been sorry abouten it, ever since. I was drunk and we was up north on a nigger shoot and we knowed it would be the last one and we was, all of us, that fired up and crazy to kill us some Black Yankees we didn't know half of what we done. I even hearn later that there was some women kilt that atternoon, and two little babies. Was that so, Shank? Was it truly so?"

It was Ira Shank's turn to let the stillness mushroom. Schlonager found himself straining forward to catch the Kansan's answer. And suddenly he found himself not so certain in his hates and supports as he had been a moment before, and he found himself wondering if Shank was feeling the same thing, a doubt, an unsureness, a least halt in his absolute indictment of the ignorant and ill-natured Confederate guerrilla.

Shank was.

"Thirteen years," he said again, and heavily. "Thirteen years, six months, seven days I've been following you, waiting and praying for the day and time when I would find you, and have you alone and in the dark and helpless as I have had you for the past half an hour—with my carbine trained on the pit of your body in this pitch darkness—thirteen years and then only to find that you don't even know what you did, and worse, you don't know why you did it. If there is a God up there above, he is not watching with us tonight. He has not been watching with me for thirteen years of nights. I don't know what to tell you, Clevenger. You're a scum and a dog and a senseless, brutal human being, but I can't kill you and I can't even hate you. You're a filth for which there is no decent word and no reasonable emotion. Yet, in your way, you're no worse than I, and no more wicked. To kill is to kill, senselessly, or deliberately. I wish to God I could have known that as clearly thirteen years ago as I know it tonight." He faded the words off and sat looking out through the darkness, and Schlonager let all the tension go out of his huge body, knowing it was over between the two men. Mudcat Clevenger, too, let down, and shook his bony head and said, convinced as ever, to Shank; "I was right. You really are daft. You're crazy as hell."

"No," said Honus Schlonager, low-voiced, and stepping forward out of the shadow of the shed's wall, "he's not crazy, Clevenger; you are: you're mad as a hydrophobia skunk, and I'm going to put you where you won't be biting nobody else for the rest of your life."

The two soldiers came to their feet, startled, and staring at him.

"You're going to do what?" growled Mudcat Clevenger.

"I'm going to put you under arrest," said Schlonager. "And when we get back to Pitchfork, I'm going to do my best to make the charge stick, and I think that with Shank for witness I can do that, and that we can put you where you won't be biting nobody but yourself, and for a long, long time."

"Charge?" rasped Clevenger, lifting his thin lip over yellow eyeteeth. "What the hell charge is that?"

"Murder," said Schlonager softly. "That Indian boy died fifteen minutes ago."

6

"THAT'S FINE," SAID MARIO SCORTINI. "I WOULDN'T want to go through that list of woes I gave you half an hour ago, but you'll remember some of them, I'm sure. Now we got Mudcat under arrest to add to the total. Honus, I sometimes wonder about you."

"Yes," said Schlonager, "so do I."

"What I wonder," explained the corporal, "is how come you got such a feel for trouble? Long as I've known you, it's been one damned thing after another. If they ain't got any grief for you, you go find your own. Like arresting this miserable hillbilly for murder. How you going to make that stick, Honus? You can't do it. For what? For killing an Indian in self-defense? It ain't Mudcat that needs a lawyer, it's you that needs a doctor."

"No," said Schlonager, "what I need is a shovel."

Scortini leaned forward in the dark, peering at him. "You going to dig for treasure?" he asked.

"What time is it?" said Schlonager.

"Ten-fifteen, why?"

"Keep care of that watch, Mario. I don't think we got another one in the detail."

"I know damned well we ain't, but what's it matter? You going to trade my turnip to them Sioux for safe passage home? Or you going to auction it off for charity? What the hell is there about this old pocket clock that needs kept care of?"

"Time," said Schlonager, "is important. It's one of the things that separates us from the animals. You got to keep track of the time. Everything runs on time."

"Sure," said Mario Scortini, with his wolfish grin. "Like the return trip to Fort Pitchfork, for instance, eh? Or our last three months' pay. Or your hitch expiring at sundown day after tomorrow, eh, Honus boy?"

"You remembered about the hitch," said Schlonager. "I had forgotten it. That's funny."

"Not for you," countered Scortini. "For you it's only normal. I never seen a man so dumb and loyal in my enlisted life."

The big sergeant looked at him and shook his head slowly. "I could never see what was so dumb about

55

being loyal," he frowned. "But then if a man isn't bright he wouldn't see it, would he?"

"No," said Scortini, coloring. "What you want the damned shovel for? I think I seen one down in the shed before it got dark. We going to trench in?"

"Only some of us."

"What's that mean?"

"The dead. We'll need their horses tomorrow."

"You going to plant them here? Tonight?"

"Yes. Get the shovel and Pulaski. Don't bother the others. I'll be in the house."

"The crazy house, I think," growled Scortini, and started off toward the stock shed.

When he had gone, Schlonager went on up to the main cabin. He stopped at the near corner of the little structure, where the glow of Squint's cigarette and the blue smoke from Harry Albion's pipe stood forth against the blackness.

"Everything all right here?" he asked.

"The accommodations are inadequate but the service is even worse," answered the Englishman. "But of course one expects these conditions in the outlands. After all, it isn't expensive, though, and the view at sunset is superb. If only the natives weren't so unfriendly."

Schlonager stared down at him. "You better get inside, Harry," he advised. "I think you've been moonstruck."

Squint Hibbard spun away his cigarette, began rolling another. "By what moon?" he asked dryly. "I

56

never seen it so black since that last night in the woods before Appomattox. By God, you not only cain't *see* your hand in front of your face, you can't even *feel* it. Mister, it's dark."

"It seems to be," agreed Schlonager.

He stood a moment and the two soldiers waited for him to say what he had come to say. The pause elongated. Finally, Harry Albion got stiffly to his feet. "Sergeant," he announced, clearing his throat, "word has come from the front lines that our regiment has been cut off and that the situation has worsened since sundown. I beg to report, sir, that Company A and Company H are ready to go forward when called upon."

Schlonager frowned, then nodded. "I take it that's *A* for Albion and *H* for Hibbard," he said.

"Yes, sir," saluted the lanky Englishman. "Ready as reported, even if not willing."

"Thanks, Harry," said Schlonager. "I only wanted to be sure you boys were awake."

"Sure," drawled Squint. "Old Mother Schlonager, you're known as. Every soldier who ever did time under you remembers being tucked in and kissed goodnight."

"There's a dirty word I'd like to apply to you right here," said Honus Schlonager, "but I don't have the strength. You'll have to wait till we get back."

Harry Albion laughed his whinnying English laugh. "I say, Sergeant," he murmured, "you really are a droll chap. If you've anything wicked or lascivious to say to me, I wish that you would favor me with its visitation more or less immediately. Somehow, I fail to share your optimism concerning the ride back. You follow me, I'm sure."

"No," said Schlonager, spreading his heavy legs and turtling his bullethead forward, "you're wrong; I don't follow you, Harry. You follow me. And we *will* get back."

"Yes, sir," said the other. "I've always deferred to the man who knows where he's going. Especially if he sports three stripes and a size eighteen collar. What was it you wanted to see us about, Sergeant?"

"Just making my rounds," growled Schlonager, and stomped on into the tiny sod-roofed shanty. Going through its low doorway, he did not stoop far enough and banged into the head timber with a force that nearly scalped him. He called on his twenty-three years eleven months and thirty days of army life for the proper curse, and rendered it with feeling. He heard Squint Hibbard and the English trooper laugh, and that didn't help. They knew, he thought. They knew damned well that he had wanted to ask them for help—to back him in this bad place—and had lost his nerve at the last moment, and stalked off angry at himself for an almost-weakness which in another sergeant would have been expected but which in Schlonager was impossible. He was getting old. There could be no doubt remaining of that. He would have to take another sight on that decision of his to sign over for his next hitch of the thirty years that would retire him with full benefits. He had better give good thought to quitting when this hitch was up two sundowns from now. August 3rd, 1877, that was the date for Honus Schlonager to be thinking about. Time had run out on him six years ahead of schedule. He wasn't fit to soldier another tour on this man's frontier.

He felt for and adjusted the wormy cowhide that covered the door, and pulled over the single twenty-inch window the flour-sack curtain that made of Mrs. Shuffman's house a home. Then he found and lit the coal-oil lamp, and waited for Scortini to come with the shovel and with the bohunkie coal miner, Casimir Pulaski.

The sod house—it was really a combination of log cabin and sod construction—consisted of one room 10 x 12 feet in size, with a half-loft 6 x 12 feet built over the north end and reached by a ladder. Since the roof was of the flat, shed type, the ceiling under the loft room was less than six feet high. In that low end of the main room were the sleeping quarters of the Shuffman couple and the wood-burning, grass-burning prairie stove which both heated the cabin and cooked its spare meals. It was no accident, Schlonager knew, that the stove was located adjacent to the sleeping arrangements, both above and below. In the bitter heart of the Wyoming winter, that added warmth emanating from the constantly stoked "hay-burner" range, made survival through the night possible. At the far end of the room, only twelve feet away, ice would freeze to the bottom of the water barrel so viciously as to burst iron cooping rings, or stout oak staves wide apart. Schlonager, examining the rude hovel, shook his head. He had seen a few of these prairie holes, and then some. But this one was as meager as they came. It made a person shrink at the idea of little kids and a decent woman living in it, and it made any man grow angry inside at the thought of any other man who would ask a woman and her children to exist in such a stable. Shuffman, no matter what Mrs. Shuffman and the young ones may have been, or were, Shuffman himself had to have been a purely no-good sort. Schlonager found himself hating and despising the dead man, and not feeling anything for the Sioux who had cut him down and taken his hair and left him still alive in the middle of the Tensleep Trail. Even, in a way, he understood how the Indians felt about Shuffman. And even, in another way, he agreed with them. So, finally, he did feel something for the Sioux who had killed Shuffman, and what he felt was a sort of sadness and sorrow that went deep and would not lie quietly.

Scortini came in past the cowhide, cursing its stink and the heat of the house behind it. Pulaski squeezed in beside him and stood blinking owlishly in the lamplight.

"*Madre!*" said the wiry corporal, "how do you stand it in here? Let's open it up; we'll strangle."

"I don't want the Indians to see what we're doing," said Schlonager. "I don't want them mutilating or cutting parts off the lieutenant or the others. That's why I'm putting them in here."

"You're *what?*" The question burst from Scortini, its import clearly too much to accept.

Schlonager reached for the shovel, taking it from the Sicilian corporal, handing it to the squat Pole, Pulaski. "We're burying them in here—inside— tonight, right now. Pulaski, start digging here." He dragged aside the rotting buffalo hide that covered the dirt floor nearly wall-to-wall of the tiny room. "I want the hole six-by-three-by-three. Pile all the dirt on this bull hide. Don't spill it around the room. You understand?"

The Pole nodded. "Sure," he said. "I like to dig."

Scortini glanced at him nervously. He didn't like the powerful miner. He said and thought that he was crazy, and he was afraid of him. "Yeah," he rasped, "I'll bet you do. Especially graves, eh? Is that it, Hunkie? Like the one you hid your wi—" Schlonager struck him with the flatted back of his hand, across the chest, driving him against the log wall. The blow was like that which an upreared grizzly would use, and Scortini had to fight to force his chest to move and the air to get back into his lungs. As he did, Schlonager said quietly to Pulaski, "You dig, I'll be back. We'll do this together, you and me. All right?" Pulaski looked up at him, pausing with the shovel embedded in the packed earth of the hut's floor. There was a peculiar look of gratitude and softness in the wild blue eyes and his voice broke croakingly.

61

"Sure," he said. "You and me, Sergeant. We'll do it."

Schlonager went out, shoving Scortini ahead of him.

Outside, the corporal began to show his Latin blood but the big German did not let him get well started.

"Mario," he said, "you were wrong. We don't know what he did to his wife. Maybe he never even had a wife. We don't know a thing about it."

Scortini spat out an obscenity. "He caved in her head with a mine pick," he said, "and stuffed her into a laundry basket and sawed off her legs and laid them in it on top of her when he couldn't get her all to go in. Then he buried the basket in a quicklime pit dug at night in his woodshed. He buried her eight feet deep in a hole that took him four days to dig. The only reason they ever caught him was that he went into town to buy a headstone for her. To put up in that woodshed! Imagine that? He's crazier than Mudcat Clevenger ever dared to be. And don't tell me we don't know anything about him. That was all in the papers that I've just said. Every damn line of it and a lot more I've forgot."

Schlonager looked at him in his slow frowning way.

"Did you see the papers?" he asked.

"Hell no, I didn't see them! I was told about them, though. It's the same thing. Everybody knows he hacked her up and dug her eight foot under!"

"No they don't, Mario. We're just talking about a story that has followed this poor devil for years. We don't know it's true; we don't know a single real thing about him."

"You," said Scortini disgustedly, "are bullheaded as a Missouri artillery mule. Come on; let's go get the bodies."

"No," said Schlonager, "I'll get them. You go stand guard with Shank over Clevenger."

"Hell, why for? Mudcat ain't going no place. I tied him so tight he can't lick his lips."

"I don't want you to guard him from getting loose; it's Shank I want you to watch."

"Shank? I thought you told me he was played out? That he wouldn't make any more trouble about Mudcat."

"Shank's a little crazy, too, Mario. Like the rest of us. I don't know for certain what he'll do, any more than he knows. He's run down for right now, but he can come on again if he gets to thinking back. When a man's mind has been twisted once, it tends to warp right back when you straighten it out. Shank's brain may curve square back to Belle Prairie any minute that he's sitting there in the dark alone with the man that shot his kid brothers and the old darkie. So watch them close. Both of them."

Scortini grinned, white teeth flashing in the outer gloom. From nowhere, he produced a knife with a nine-inch blade and a Bowie blood channel. He palmed its haft, rolled the weapon, sheathed it with the same invisible motion he had brought it forth.

"Yes sir," he said, saluting. "I may even do better than that. I may take care of the whole thing for you and Shank and Mudcat and the army. Who knows?"

63

"I'll know," said Schlonager. "I've seen the mark of that pocket saber before. Just watch them, Mario."

"Sure, sure," said the other, fading off into the night toward the murky outline of the stock shed. "I can't understand why you never learned to trust me . . ."

7

WHEN SCHLONAGER NEARED THE BODIES A LIGHT WIND stirred above them and came to him. He recoiled involuntarily. The full day beneath the broiling sun and the hours-long blowing by the flies had brought the corpses to a puffed and spoiling state that struck through the dark like a physical blow. The stench was no worse, either, than the swollen feel of them. But Schlonager took them one by one over his shoulder and bore them up to the sod house and lay them by its door, handling them tenderly as though they yet held life, or some chance to live. It was the way he felt about fellow soldiers who fell in the field. He knew it was a foolish thing and was glad it was dark. Others would not understand.

Inside the tiny cabin Pulaski already had his hole trenched out for dimension and was a foot down into the rammed earth of the floor. He swung the shovel as though it were a weapon, powering the dirt upward onto the buffalo hide in surging, grunting strokes that seemed, literally, to open the grave by visible suction. Schlonager waited for him to finish, resting his broad back against the front wall near the door. Presently, the Pole straightened. He had dug to a depth above his knees. He did not measure this amount, nor question Schlonager about it. He nodded merely to himself and said out loud, "She deep enough," and climbed out of the hole.

Without a word more, he began to follow Schlonager outside to help bring in the bodies, but the big German laid a hand on his shoulder and told him, no, that he would ask no man to do this other work. Pulaski shrugged and stood as ordered. If he appreciated the gesture, the gratitude failed to show in his brutish face. Schlonager got the four corpses laid into the ground, packing them alternately like tinned fish, head and tail, so that they would fit into the narrow, shallow tomb. The limbs were stiff, some of them, and would not lie well or closely. He had to put his boot into them and grind them into wrenching obedience. Pulaski, watching, showed no emotion. When the cadavers were at last forced to rest peacefully by Schlonager's hand and foot, he came forward and reached for the shovel stuck in the mound of earth on the bull hide. Schlonager said nothing but the Pole hesitated at grave's edge looking at him, the shovel poised. Schlonager returned the look, gathered his fatigued thoughts, decided to try for the sake of the other's religion.

"Dear Lord," he said, letting his shoulders go slack and his long arms hang wearily at his sides, "these men were soldiers and died today with no chance to fight. I think all of them were good soldiers, though, and—" He trailed the words off awkwardly, extremely conscious of Pulaski's frowning, intent gaze and slowly wagging head. He wanted to curse the Pole and rage at him that he didn't know what to say and didn't care if nothing were said, and felt, for his own part, that dead men didn't know and couldn't care either. Then he remembered his own foolishness in being gentle with the way he carried them to the door. And, looking again at Pulaski, he thought he saw the dumb pleading behind the fixed stare the Pole was holding him with, and he reached desperately far back into boyhood and a fleeting memory of some words that remained from his grandfather's funeral in the Wisconsin farm settlement of his birth. "Dust to dust, ashes to ashes," he said, "dust thou art, to dust returneth—Amen . . ."

It wasn't quite right, he felt, but it was right enough. He saw the grateful gleam in Pulaski's wide blue eyes, and there was no mistaking the relief with which the squat Pole crossed himself and began to throw the earth into the grave. When the floor level was reached, Schlonager began to tamp the earth by stomping upon it. He could not help but think of the faces of the dead men so near below his boots, but there was no help for that. Soon, the grave would hold no more and the floor had been returned almost to its original appearance. "Pick up your end of the bull hide," Schlonager said to the Pole. "We'll carry the excess out in a possum-belly and dump it in the creek." Pulaski said nothing, gathered and raised his end of the hide. Together, he and the powerful German sergeant straightened. Carefully, with set teeth and straining arms and legs, they bore the heavy load down to the side of the small stream where it backed up and ran deep at its confluence with the Big Horn River. The edge was of rock, the undercurrent strong and swift. Only seconds after the earth was spilled into the water, no trace of it was to be seen either on bank or bottom of Gooseberry Creek. "All right," said Honus Schlonager, "come on; don't let the bull hide touch going back."

In the sod-house cabin Schlonager found the Shuffman woman's broom and used its crude beargrass fibers to sweep out the last traces of the common grave and to blend the outlines of the digging back into the original floor lines. When he had done what he could, he replaced the buffalo hide precisely as it had been before, Pulaski helping him.

"I don't think they will look for them in here," he told the Pole. "Maybe they wouldn't have bothered anyway; I don't know. Maybe I'm just a little old, and tired."

Pulaski looked at him and shook his head.

"I like you," was all he said.

Schlonager, somehow, felt refreshed. He grinned at the simple-minded remark but at the same time it lifted him up. Why in God's name he should care that Casimir Pulaski liked him, he could not explain. But it was in his own straight nature that he did not seek far to learn. If the big dumb cluck was ready to believe they had done the right thing in burying the lieutenant and the three men, fine, let him believe it. At nearing midnight of this stifling August day, there was little time left for any of them to believe in anything. Schlonager put his hand to the Pole's thick bicep, gave it a clumsy squeeze and pat. "Sure," he said, "we're old soldiers, Pulaski," and let it rest at that, satisfied.

There remained the matter of the Indian boy.

"Pulaski," he said, "go and get me that Sioux pony." The Pole nodded and went away through the dark, returning moments later with the nervous mustang and its silent burden. Schlonager felt the Sioux youth's body. He took its hand, raised the arm, flexed it. "He's beginning to set," he said, "I'll have to step on it." Pulaski peered at the dead Indian. He bent over and looked hard into the chiseled features of the dark face. He ran his rough hand along the sleek, cold arm and shoulder. "What are you doing?" said Schlonager sharply. The other straightened, embarrassed. "Just patting him," he said. There was a pause, then he added, "I get the shovel," and started back into the cabin. "Wait," ordered Schlonager. "I don't want the shovel." Pulaski stopped, frowning briefly. "You don't want shovel? How you bury this boy; in the creek?"

Schlonager shook his head.

"No, no, nothing like that. You never mind. Just tell Scortini I've gone to take care of Crow Mane. He'll know."

"All right," said Pulaski. "You wait here; I will be right back."

"What the devil do you mean? You're not going any place."

"You wouldn't let me?"

"Let you what? What's the matter with you? Where do you think you want to go? You getting spooked, Pulaski?"

"No, sir," said the Pole, hanging his head. "Pulaski is not afraid tonight. But I would like to go, if you say."

"You mean, go with me? To bury this Indian boy?"

"Yes, that's it."

"But why?" Schlonager was stumped. He was wondering if Scortini wasn't right after all, and this powerful, big-shouldered gnome of a bohunkie coal miner the ghoul that the little Sicilian corporal said he was. "Why in God's name would you want to do that? Haven't you had enough graveyard shift for one night?"

Pulaski continued to stand with his head down. After a moment he raised his head and moved over to the body of Crow Mane once more and stroked it gently, as before. "I liked him too," he said low-voiced to Schlonager. "And he was your friend."

The massive German soldier stared down at him. It was a strange time to discover that a man had something inside him other than fear and hatred of his fellows. He had had Pulaski over a year at Fort Pitchfork, and had never spoken more than six words in a string to him in that time. Now, of a sudden, and with other, far smarter men beginning to show cracks all around their rawing edges, this stupid coal-pit Pole was steadying down and holding like a rock.

"Well," he answered softly, "it looks like I win one and lose one. Come on."

They set off, Schlonager leading the Sioux pony, Pulaski walking beside it, his hand on Crow Mane's body to keep it in position across the mustang's saddle. After they had crossed the creek and were climbing the rock ridge beyond it, to the south, he said suddenly, "Sergeant, what you mean?" Schlonager, tired to the point of desperation, stopped squarely in the trail. He turned on the other soldier.

"Damn you," he said, "what the hell do you mean, 'what did I mean'? You're wearing me down, Pulaski. It's like trying to talk to a dog."

Pulaski nodded patiently, as though he understood the sergeant's problem, and had heard it many times phrased in the same insulting terms.

"Yes," he said, "I know. But what I mean is when you say back there you win one and lose one. What does that mean, I ask?"

Schlonager didn't get it for a moment, then it struck him. He cursed mutteringly, and helplessly.

"You mad?" said the Pole anxiously.

"No," said Schlonager quickly, "I'm not mad, Pulaski; you are." He paused, wagging his close-cropped, round head in mixed exasperation and gratitude. "What I meant back there was that in losing one friend, Crow Mane, I was gaining another friend, Casimir Pulaski." Again, he paused, this time long enough to step toward the Pole and fix him with a straight stare. "And what I mean, now," he added quickly, "is that I'm glad enough for the exchange. You understand that, you thickhead bohunkie?"

"No," said Pulaski. "Maybe not."

"I mean," said Honus Schlonager, "that I'm glad you like me, and that I consider you my friend, and that I want you to think of me as your friend. Now is that all right?"

Schlonager had never seen the Pole smile before. He felt that it was an effort for the awkward miner; something he had to stop and think about, to go back a long way and remember how it was done. But it was a smile, and Casimir Pulaski meant it all the way for a smile, even including the quick tears that went with it and that shone in the starlight, swiftly, like small and winking jewels, gone in the moment of their birth, but leaving behind them a feeling of goodness and warmth and gratefulness that would go with Sergeant Honus Schlonager a very long time past this fumbling moment midway of Gooseberry Ridge above Big Horn River and the homestead of the Shuffman widow.

"Sure," said Pulaski, "I think so."

And he and Schlonager went on up the ridge, the one ahead of, the other by the side of the little Indian mustang, and neither saying any more.

8

"WHAT DO YOU SUPPOSE THEY ARE DOING?" ASKED Little Killer. "They don't bury their dead that way, do they?"

His companion to the right shook his head.

"No, I don't think they do. But that's a very big fire; just like a burning fire, I think."

"Hmmm," said Little Killer. "What do you think, Tashunka?" he asked the brave to his left.

Tashunka Luza, Quick Horse, scowled and peered harder at the mounting blaze upon the opposite ridge. "I think we had better ride a little closer, then sneak up and make sure what they are up to. You know you can't trust a white man, and I see at least two of them over there by that fire."

The second Sioux nodded. "That sounds like a good idea," he agreed. "Falling Leaf thinks with you."

"I don't know," worried Little Killer. "It's risky going around in the night."

"Bah!" said Quick Horse. "You are an old woman. That talk of spirits in the dark is nonsense. If you had been to the school at Pine Ridge, as I have, you would know all about such foolishness. There's no ghosts around."

"Sure," said Falling Leaf, "that the talk of the old Sioux. We know better nowadays."

"I don't," insisted Little Killer. "And it was I to whom Crow Mane gasped out his last words before

72

he fell this sunset, saying for me to take charge of the war party."

"I heard him," admitted Quick Horse, "but this thing of being afraid of the spirits who come back when the sun goes is ridiculous. If you don't want to go, Falling Leaf and I will be glad to do it for you."

"Because I am cautious does not make me afraid," said Little Killer. "Remember, I am older than the rest of you and I know the white man better, and from a long ways back. I was with Crazy Horse at the Fetterman Fight. I was with Gall on the Rosebud. I was with American Horse when he—"

"*Ih!*" exclaimed Falling Leaf, "no speeches, please. I am going with Quick Horse. Are you coming?"

"Certainly," said Little Killer, turning for his pony. "Was there any question, at all, that I would not do so?"

"Never!" said Falling Leaf piously. "Were you not with Gall on the Rosebud, American Horse on the Tongue River, Hump, when he struck at Miles in the snow, Two Moons, when his Cheyenne were caught by Mackenzie, Crazy Horse at the—"

"Curse you!" flared Little Killer. "Another word and I'll give you the butt of my lance. Enough is enough. You are a great talker, we all know that. Shut up."

"*Ay-yiy-yiy!*" cried the other. "*I* am a great talker? Look who is calling whom a great talker! I appeal to you, Tashunka! Rescue me!"

"And I appeal to you," said Quick Horse shortly.

"Do what Taopi has said, Wahpeton: shut up."

"Oh, well," sulked the tall brave, "if that is the way it is going to be, all right. Two against one is white man's fun."

Neither the short, gross Quick Horse, nor the thin, wasp-smallish Little Killer replied to his lament, and the three rode quickly through the night toward the distant ridge beyond the clearing where Shuffman had built his house, and from which his woman and the three children had so mysteriously disappeared that afternoon.

When they had left their ponies in the river timber and climbed the sparsely wooded ridge atop which the fire burned, the three Sioux crept as far inward toward the blaze as they dared and lay up in the rocks, peering intently. What they saw narrowed their slant eyes. The white men *were* bidding goodbye to the dead. But not their own dead.

The funeral pyre was constructed in the precise pattern of the Dakota Sioux. It had the four corner posts set in the earth. It had the platform bearing the body built of cross sticks on bull-pine saplings. It had the cremating fire laid in interlaced, heavy stoking style, so that the flames would burn both high and long, destroying all that was mortal of the dead and freeing his spirit, cleansed by the fire, for the journey to Wanagi Yata, the Gathering Place of the Shadows. By the side of the pyre, only far enough from it to avoid damage, was tethered the sorrel paint pony of Crow Mane, the Younger. None of the watching Sioux would have thought a white man could build so perfect a replica of a Dakota burning platform. Were it not for the evidence of their own startled gazes, they would have fought any liar who had tried to tell them that here the giant white man, Schlonager, had raised and fired in honor of his dead Sioux friend, Crow Mane, the funeral pyre of his people, the one erected only in memory of the warrior who had fallen to the foe with the highest courage and Indian pride. But one had to accept the evidence of his senses. There stood the huge chevron soldier whom Crow Mane had saluted and talked with at sunset. There stood the Pony Soldier sergeant who had lived in the lodge of Crow Mane's family. Who had eaten the hump ribs and roast tongue supplied by Crow Mane's parents. Who had been nursed to health from his wounds by Crow Mane's quiet, doe-shy sister Anpetuwi, whose Sioux name meant Sunlight and whose smile was the reason for the name. There he stood, in the proper Sioux attitude, his great round head bowed, his thick arms held straight outward and upward toward the pyre's platform and the burning body of his friend who had been so treacherously lured by his soft words and then murdered by the rifle fire of his hidden soldier, among the bodies of the dead soldiers across the horses, down there in the pines past the cabin at sunset.

There he stood. The traitor. The killer. The liar.

The three Sioux looked at one another. In their dark eyes was hatred of this big man. And yet there was something else there, too. One could not see a white man pay this honor to a red man and not know some feeling other than hate. Was it possible the silver-haired sergeant had not ordered the trap? Could it have been that the hidden soldier was not his planning? That he was not placed among the dead men to pay back the Sioux for using those stuffed brown hawks that morning in the Cottonwood Rocks to kill those three Pony Soldiers and that one young Pony Soldier chief? But, no. That was open and honest warfare. It had been conducted with honor and by the rules. An ambush in broad daylight and carried off with such tremendous skill as that of the stuffed hawks had been carried off by Little Killer, whose brilliant conception it was, was a thing of pride and valor. Particularly, was it not to be held as treachery. Not when it had been performed against an old and clever soldier like Schlonager. But this thing of a man pretending to be a dead body, hanging from a horse all the way across the basin from the river bluff, being left across his horse among the standing horses that carried the real dead bodies of the other soldiers— bah! this was miserable and cowardly and, worse, it was something unclean.

Thoughts tending in this direction crossed the minds of all three silent Indian watchers of that funeral burning in the honor of Crow Mane, the Younger. Thinking them, the dark faces grew darker. And yet, and yet . . .

Over by the pyre, Schlonager was unfolding his

arms. He was bending and picking up in his left hand a scooping of the rocky dust of the ridge. He was taking pinches of it in the fingers of his right hand and tossing them into the air in the four cardinal directions of Mother Maka, the Earth. And they could plainly hear his deep voice intoning the correct and sacred Sioux words for the last farewell.

"Tunka sila le iyahpe ya yo . . . Father, receive my offering. Take you this brave man who comes to you in pride and humbleness. Lead you his pony where the grass is deep and the water swift and clean. Make him happy, make him content. Show him where the sun is shining. Keep him with you, as I have kept him with me, in your heart."

The prayer ended, Schlonager raised his head and dropped his tired arms. The other white man, the ugly one with bent shoulders and hanging arms long to his knees, made a sign like the Black Robe Fathers made, with his fingers on his breast, like a cross, and also raised his head and put down his hands from signing the cross.

"We can go, I think," he said loudly to Schlonager.

"Yes," answered the big sergeant. "He will burn now. We might as well get down the ridge while we can. Most Sioux are against night traveling, but you don't want to bet your hair on it."

"What?" asked the slow, stupid man.

"Crow Mane's friends," answered the sergeant. "They might see the fire and come to see what we're cooking."

The other shook his head. "I don't think," he said.

Schlonager grinned, weary as he was. "You sure don't, Pulaski," he said. "But I do, and that's what counts, eh? Come on; let's move out."

They went off, angling down the slope by the trail they had come up. Thirty paces along it, they passed beneath an overhang of boulders and base rock which shadowed the path no more than ten feet above them. The crouching Sioux, each with knife, short lance or war ax to hand, could have killed them as certainly as though they were two sheep, or two cows, going along to water or to grass and not watching out for bear or panther or wolf lain up in the rocks above.

But the Indians did not move.

Once more they seemed to speak to one another with wordless looks of their gleaming dark eyes, and to agree upon the exchange. It was only after the white men had gone on past them and were surely out of earshot down the hill, that one of them—it was Falling Leaf—broke the stillness.

"Well," he said, "I am wondering if you others are thinking what I am thinking?"

"I think we are," nodded Quick Horse. "What do you say, Taopi?"

Little Killer inclined his head gravely, and announced thoughtfully, "Let me say it and then we shall see if it is what you have in your own minds. I am thinking that we must honor that old sergeant, too. That we must do the same thing for him that he has done for our young chief. I am thinking that we will build him a platform also. Am I right, cousins?"

"Yes," said Falling Leaf, "you are just right."

"It is so," concluded Quick Horse. "We will kill this Schlonager and burn his body in full honor. Could we do less for him than he has done for us?"

"Never," said Falling Leaf. "*Hopo,* let's go!"

"*Hookahey!*" growled Little Killer. "To the horses—!"

9

"HONUS, IT'S TIME."

Scortini shook the big sergeant with rough gentleness. Schlonager responded slowly. The fatigue had been so deep upon him that to emerge from it, even after four hours' sleep, was like recovering from chloroform surgery. "All right," he mumbled, "all right . . ." and was asleep again.

"Honus, damn it, wake up!" Scortini rasped the words now. "It's getting light over east. Hell, it *is* light!"

Schlonager groaned and sat up.

"What time is it?" he asked.

Scortini consulted his pocket watch, scratching and cupping a match to see its face. "Four-thirty," he said.

"Is everything all quiet out yonder?"

"You mean the Indians or our heroes?"

"Both."

"Well, no sign of the Sioux, Mudcat's still tied up, Shank ain't recoiled his brain yet and Pulaski is still snoring. I don't know about Squint and Harry."

"You don't need to worry about them."

"I hope not; we got other problems of a pressing nature. Like you going out before it gets any lighter and scouting to make sure the Indians ain't snuck into the local timber during the night."

Schlonager nodded and got stiffly to his feet. "God," he said, "a man surely does grow old. That's my first night on the ground this year. It liked to killed me."

"I hope," said the Sicilian corporal, "that when I'm your age I can be as old as you are. They broke the tough mold after they poured you, Honus. *Santa!*"

Schlonager only nodded again. The motion was a dismissal of the compliment, not an agreement to its sense. "I won't be gone long," he said. "Just going to look over that clump of bull pine where Mudcat got the boy, and then the brush along the creek. Twenty minutes, likely."

"Anything special you want me to do while you're out?"

"Yes, you better check Shank and Mudcat again. With Pulaski asleep up here—well, I still think we've got to watch Shank. He's a peculiar devil. Too reasonable about everything, if you know what I mean."

"No," said Scortini, "I ain't the least notion what you mean. Me, I'd be keeping the evil eye on Clevenger. But every man to his own poison. I'll check Shank. Be careful out there, Daniel Boone."

Schlonager paused, bending down to peer at his

diminutive fellow soldier. "I'm always careful," he answered. "It's the secret of my charm."

"I always knew something was," nodded Scortini, with his evil grin. "But the way you keep a secret, who would know?"

"Me," said Honus Schlonager, and started away through the half dark of the coming day.

In the woods along the course of Gooseberry Creek and in the clumping of pine where the Sioux had caught them the past sunset, there was no sign of the hostiles. On the flanks of the rocky ridge beyond the creek, he noticed a hatch of early rising sage sparrows hopping and flitting over something attractive on the ground. Going swiftly upward to the place, he found pony droppings which were still soft and, when broken open, faintly warm in the center.

He looked toward the ridge top and the funeral platform of Crow Mane. The scaffolding poles still stood but the pyre proper had burned down and with it had gone the body of the young Sioux chief. Smoke still rose from the pile of ashes between the upright saplings. Schlonager nodded.

"They must have been close enough to touch us," he told himself, "yet they didn't. Why?"

He would like to have gone up to the top and gotten some answers. Such as how many of them had come over to watch the fire, which way they had departed, and if all that had come over had gone back. But it was already too light. By the time he went up the ridge and back he would be exposed enough for a long rifle shot, let alone for a close one, say, from just beyond the ridge. He drifted quickly back to the creek, crossed it and went up to the cabin in the clearing. Scortini was waiting for him.

"Anything?" asked the corporal.

"No," said Schlonager. "How about you?"

"Nothing," answered Scortini. "I found Shank asleep. It was his watch but I didn't climb him about it. Mudcat was wide awake. Pulaski's still snoring."

Schlonager braced his shoulders, took a deep breath.

"Well," he said, "I guess that brings us right down to it. I wish I knew where to start."

"Start?" frowned Scortini. "Start what?"

"Looking for Mrs. Shuffman and the kids."

"Oh, come on now, Honus, they're not around here! Are you going to believe that damned Indian of yours? He was dying, for God's sake. And he was a Sioux."

"Exactly," said Honus Schlonager. "They like to die clean and true. He knew that he was going; that's why he told me about not finding the woman or the kids."

"Of course!" sneered Scortini. "You see, I've only known you about a hundred years or so, and I never really understood your deep and devoted love for the red brother. Not up until right now, anyway. You can't be serious, Honus. Or maybe you can. I guess I'm like Mudcat; I haven't had enough sleep."

Schlonager swept his hand around the clearing, the arc of the motion going from river bluff to the Big Horn and back to river bluff.

82

"Somewhere inside that three-quarter circle," he said, "that woman and those kids are hid out. I know it. They have got to be. That's what Crow Mane was telling me."

"I heard what he said," challenged Scortini. "I didn't hear any such of a thing as that."

"I did," insisted Schlonager obstinately. "The question is, *where?*"

"Where, *what?*" demanded his companion irritably.

"That woman," said Schlonager, "and those three little kids; where at are they hiding?"

"*Maria!*" growled Scortini, raising both hands helplessly. "I give up!"

"I'd like to," said Schlonager, "but I can't."

"And why not?" grumbled the other man. "You got some special dispensation from the Pope, or something, says you got to keep looking for something which ain't no longer to be found, or that calls on you to risk all our necks to scout this Sioux pasture till you turn up certain signs them red devils killed the family, or run off with them, or fifty-fifty, or whatever?"

"No," said the older man, leaning wearily against the cabin wall, "all I've got are my orders."

"Your *orders!*" snorted Scortini derisively.

"Yes," said Honus Schlonager, "to find and bring in a sod-house widow woman and three kids. You know what that means to me, Mario?"

The little corporal grimaced, his monkey's face contorted in an expression of dismay compounded by sheer exasperation.

"Yes, sir, Sergeant Schlonager," he said resignedly, "I know exactly what that means to you; *to find and bring in a sod-house widow woman and three kids:* Hail Mary, amen, and go to hell!"

"Something like that," said Schlonager. "You got any idea where to start looking?"

"Sure," said Scortini, "wherever the buzzards are circling."

10

"IF YOU WERE THAT WOMAN, WHERE WOULD YOU HIDE?" said Schlonager.

"In the timber of the creek, or the river, or the rocks and scrub of the ridges." Scortini palmed his hands. "In this God-forsaken country there's nowhere else to hide."

"Not the river," said Schlonager. "It's too far from the house. And it's too low down there. No place for a hole. She must be in a hole somewhere. But where?"

"Why a hole?"

"It's the way people are when they want to hide, that's all. It's like when you're hurt you want to get under a roof. Same with when you want to hide. You want to crawl in a hole."

"You're smart," said Scortini. "I wouldn't want you to be looking for me. Not if I didn't want to have you find me." He paused, and Schlonager nodded. "That's an idea," he said. "She may not want us to find her.

84

She may be afraid of anybody—everybody—by this time. People get wild when the Indians are around. Women most of all."

"Sure," said Scortini, "they got the most reason to."

"It depends . . ." said Schlonager, and fell to thinking. After several minutes, during which his blue-gray eyes went over and over and over the circle from the bluffs to the Big Horn and back, he bobbed his round head. "She ought to be somewhere along the creek. Not up it, for there it thins in its timber and goes to rock and scrub, and you can see it too well. Down the creek, that's where. Nearly where Pulaski and I dumped the dirt in. Down by the river." His face brightened. "Yes, that's it!" he said. "In the clay bluff about four feet above the waterline there's a wolf hole. I saw it this morning. Just dimly and not thinking of it, then. But that's the place."

"You're balmy," said Scortini. "How could she get to it without her and the kids' tracks showing on the bank? You were just down there. You didn't say anything about any tracks."

"No, there weren't any tracks. That gives us the next question; how did she get in there without going along the bank?"

"My God!" exploded the corporal, "go back to sleep and get some more rest. You don't even know there's a real hole there. You don't even know that, if there is a hole, this woman and her kids is in it, or a damned thing. Yet you're worrying about how they got there! Well, hell, I'll tell you how they did it.

Secret passage, of course! They just tunneled under the meadow. Why, shucks, it would be easy. It ain't over a hundred and fifty feet from the cabin to the creek bank. They could make a tunnel like that in, oh, say, six years if they stayed with it. Maybe seven if—"

"That's it!" cried Schlonager. "That has got to be it. But not from the cabin, Mario, the shed! They've tunneled to the bank from the stock shed! Look down there."

Scortini did as he was told, not because he wanted to, or thought any the less that the old sergeant was feeling the strain. But, as he looked, he began to think and to see what Schlonager was talking about.

That shed was seventy-five feet from the house. They had discussed the strangeness of that previously—why a man in Indian country would build his horse barn so far from his house. Now, perhaps, shrewd old Honus Schlonager had smelled out the reason. It could not be over twenty-five or thirty feet to the creek bluff from the shed's interior. Somewhere in that wind-leaned structure, between the two stalls and the wagon space and the tiny feed and harness compartment, there had to be a trap door—according to Schlonager. And Schlonager, old, tired, worn out or whatever, was still a hard bear to corner. He was still Schlonager.

"All right," said the corporal, "let's go see."

Rounding the corner of the cabin, they paused to talk with Harry Albion, taking the dawn guard while his companion, Squint Hibbard, slept. Near them, along the cabin wall, Pulaski lay stretched as though dead, heavy chest heaving uneasily to give the only lie to the impression.

"Harry," said Schlonager, "are you all right here?" When the Englishman had indicated that they were, he added, "We're going down to the shed. Wake up Pulaski and have him take a post by the front door. I've been out earlier and found no sign of the Sioux coming in closer during the night." Harry Albion nodded and asked quickly, "Did you see any sign of them at all, Sergeant?" Schlonager told him of the fresh pony droppings and his idea that he and Pulaski had been allowed to live during their burning of the young chief. "That," said the Englishman, "is bloody strange. What do you make of it?" "Nothing," replied Schlonager, "except that they are still around. I'd hoped they would scatter and keep drifting after Mudcat downed Crow Mane. But we're not being mired down with luck this trip, eh?" To this, Albion nodded once more. "Not quite," he said. "Anything else, Sergeant?" Schlonager shook his head. "Just stay awake," he said.

He and Scortini went on across the open clearing to the shed. Nearing it, they both got the feeling that it was too quiet, and assumed the two soldiers had fallen asleep. But they were wrong. Only one of them had fallen asleep, and it was a sleep from which he would never awaken. Ira Shank was dead, his skull split like a dropped melon by a rear blow with a weapon that still lay among the musty debris of the shed floor, the Kansan's blood and black hair still clotting its rusted tug eye. The prisoner, Mudcat Clevenger, was gone. In some way he had slashed free his bonds, secured the shard of broken whiffletree, crept up behind his guard and killed him with one vicious slash of the iron-capped hickory club. Shank's Spencer Carbine was gone with Mudcat. Scortini and Schlonager exchanged glances and stood motionless over the corpse of the vengeful Jayhawker. The idea of Mudcat being loose with a gun and belt of ammunition was not a pleasant nor a promising one. The prospect of Shank's death having reduced their small number by one good soldier was, if possible, an even grimmer vista. It was Honus Schlonager who moved first.

"Well," he said, letting his hunched shoulders ease, "I guess he's not in here, or we wouldn't be. I think, by now, we've got him to where he'll shoot on sight."

"That's right." Scortini too eased upright from his fearful crouch over the body of the murdered man. "If he was still in here we wouldn't be talking about it. Question is, where the hell did he get to? Harry's been awake up yonder since before daybreak. He'd have seen him break for the woods or the river, after I left the shed on my last check. Hell, it was getting daylight then."

"Mario," said Schlonager, who had been frowning in hard thought while the corporal worried out loud, "look sharp around in here—you notice anything been moved?"

Scortini darted his black eyes around the shed. His glance fastened on a pile of hay, loosely rolled in bundles and tied with twine after the frontier fashion, which lay against the rear wall of the harness cubicle. He looked silently at the sergeant, who nodded, and the two glided toward the spot. But when they had pounced upon the hay pile they found no harvest of humanity beneath it. It merely gave to their combined weights and, when subsequently moved bundle by bundle away from the wall, showed nothing beneath it but the dirt floor of the shed. The two soldiers stood up, looking foolish and feeling more nervous than ever.

"Bad guess," said Scortini. "But something had moved that hay around."

"It was him," said Schlonager, "but why? What was he looking for? Not just a place to hide when he heard us coming. Nothing that desperate and unthought out. Not with Shank lying dead long enough for his blood to crust."

"No," said Scortini, "that's so. But then what was he doing over here stirring the hay bundles around?"

"Looking for something," said the other.

"Sure, but what?"

"Something he saw. Or thought he saw."

"Like what?"

"Like a way out of here without crossing the meadow."

Scortini stared at him. "You mean he found what me and you come down here to look for? The way to the wolf hole in the creek bank? Honus, you're worse off for want of sleep than I figured."

"Something led him to it," said Schlonager. "What?"

Again he studied the shed. "That oat bin," he pointed to the hasp-lidded feedbox built against the wall next to the piled hay, "we looked in that before. It was empty, wasn't it? I mean, except for a few handfuls of loose oats."

"Yeah, that's right. A few loose oats and a little seed corn, mixed. Just the usual leavings. He probably used it to store his seed and feed both in—Shuffman, I mean. That's why he had it built of finished lumber with tinned corners, to keep the rats and mice from his seed."

Schlonager, shaking his head, moved to the oat bin. He stood over it, staring down at it. Presently, he once more raised the fitted lid. The rusted hinges squealed harshly, and were still. So was Honus Schlonager, his broad face suddenly tense, his warm blue eyes narrowed warningly.

"Mario," he said softly, "come here."

The corporal moved to his side and peered into the opened bin. For a moment he showed no emotion, then his dark face writhed and he looked up at Schlonager.

"No oats, no corn," he whispered. "Not even a hull or a kernel. She's clean as if she'd been dumped."

"She *has* been dumped!" said Schlonager with rare excitement. "That's a false bottom to that bin, Mario—there's our wolf-hole entrance, for certain!"

The Sicilian corporal nodded, dark eyes glitteringly cold. "Yeah," he said, "and there's where our wolf has just disappeared on his way to den up with your widow woman and her three cubs."

Schlonager straightened, closing the lid carefully. His face had gone a fish-gray color. By his sides, his huge hands slowly knotted and unknotted themselves.

"God," he said hoarsely, "I'd for a minute forgot her and them. . . ."

11

MUDCAT DOZED FITFULLY. HE WANTED TO STAY AWAKE and he fought the sleep like an enemy. When Mario Scortini had come in just now to check on him and his guard, Mudcat had been nearly asleep. But he had heard the corporal coming and had gotten his eyes open in time to see who it was and to be relieved that it wasn't the sergeant. He had been decent to Scortini and they had exchanged a few meaningless words. He didn't hate the little dago corporal, he told himself. It was only the thickheaded kraut sergeant that he had to get. That Honus Schlonager. That big beefy-handed devil with the iron head and strength of a bear or a buffalo. He was the one. Get past him and you were a free man. Nobody else in that scummy patrol of cowards and fools would come after him. No, they weren't yellow, either, he decided. They weren't any more yellow than he was. But they were fools. Every one of them. And he was not a fool. Not Mudcat Clevenger. If he could only get loose. Only get something sharp or ragged to work his bonds against. He had to do it. Had to find some way . . .

But the tiredness of two nights awake came on him again and his head dropped. This time it was not outer footsteps that awakened him. Something was moving *inside* the shed. Clevenger did not stir. The only thing that twitched about his slumped form was the lid of his right eye coming halfway open. Dimly, to his right, he saw the small form. It was a little boy of perhaps seven or eight years of age. He was a shaggy towhead, barefooted and dressed in the rags of the frontier sod-house poor. He crouched and stepped as warily, though, as any Indian or white-trash swamp boy of Mudcat's own Southern Missouri River boyhood memories. Indeed, he reminded Mudcat of himself thirty years before, and for a moment the lanky guerrilla was swayed by nostalgia and some feeling of hopeful kindred with the wild-looking sod-house boy. But then he saw the knife at the lad's waist, and all other feelings were swept under in his hunger for the keen blade.

Still he did not move. The boy was creeping past him and the sleeping Shank to get to the open face of the shed where he might look up toward the cabin and after the departing figure of Corporal Scortini.

Mudcat let him go, his mind churning for a way to use him, to get him to come closer and to gain his confidence . . . and his knife.

While the boy paused at the shed opening, looking out over the clearing and up toward the soldiers at his crude home of logs and sods, Mudcat tried to see past the partition that divided the harness room from the rest of the shed. But all he could make out was the pile of bundled hay rolls that showed above the top of the low divider. That seemed enough, though. He thought the boy must have escaped the Indians by hiding under the hay, while his mother and the other two children had been captured or killed. He must have lain there all through the dark of the past night, not knowing what to do and fearing the sound of the soldiers' voices as much as the guttural gruntings of the red men. No, damn it, that wouldn't hold water either. The kid would not have stayed there all night. Not when he heard white men talking. No, there was something funny about where that kid had come from. Something mighty odd and fishy. But it could wait. It had to wait. The thing now was the knife. And the boy was turning from the opening, now, his look at the cabin and the cavalrymen finished. Studying his face, Mudcat could see it had changed since his examination of the cabin and the clearing. It had lost its drawn fear and was showing hope and a sort of eagerness which had not been showing on it before. That boy was thinking those soldiers were there to save him and he was going now toward Ira Shank, on tiptoe, with the positively clear intention of waking him up and letting him know that the patrol had come in time to save at least one of the Shuffman brood. That boy was going to wake up Shank, and with that waking up, he was going to ruin the last shred of a chance that Mudcat Clevenger might have remaining to get himself set free and so given a decent shot at staying alive. If that boy got to Shank, Mudcat Clevenger would go into Fort Pitchfork a prisoner of Sergeant Honus Schlonager. And dead witness or no dead witness, Mudcat did not care, nor dare, to risk his word against that of the oldest regular army sergeant in Wyoming. *He had to move.*

"Kid!" he whispered desperately, "don't touch that feller! Leave him lay there. You know what he is?"

The boy wheeled about to face him. He started to run, then stopped. He looked at the sleeping Shank, then at the grinning, friendly Missourian. He got curious when he saw that Mudcat was tied up. He came a little nearer, craning his head, knees bent, holding back, ready either to fly or be friendly, but in either event showing the deadly interest of small boys the world over in mysterious circumstances wherein seemingly nice men were being hurt or treated sadly by others. Mudcat saw the advantage and pressed it.

"Boy," he said, just shading a whisper, "these here devils are rennygades, you know what that means?"

The boy shook his head, big-eyed.

"Outlaw killers," said Mudcat. "They jumped my patrol of soldiers from Fort Pitchfork and tooken our uniforms and kilt all the men but me, which they saved to use for a hostage—you know, to trade with, or suchlike."

The boy nodded, still saying nothing.

"Now," Mudcat went on, "don't make a sound, nor even breathe loud, and maybe you and me kin get outen here alive. Understand, boy?"

Again the youth bobbed his shaggy blond head.

"You cut me loose," said Mudcat, "and I'll help you to get away with me. I know the way to Fort Pitchfork. We kin make it there and get the real soldiers to come back and catch these here murdering rennygades. Come on, we got to hurry."

The boy eased his knife from the rope belt which held up both it and his ragged trousers. "How about my maw and Marybell and the baby?" he asked soberly.

"We'll take 'em along," promised Mudcat unhesitatingly. "Now cut me loose, boy, before that devil wakes up and kills us both!"

The child moved, still uncertainly, toward Clevenger. He stopped and reached toward him with the knife, knowing some instinctive doubts but acting as a boy will when directed by a grown man with force and persuasive threat of danger. As the blade sliced through the doubled ropes and Mudcat's thick wrists fell apart and were freed, the boy moved back with the quick uneasiness and poised curiosity of the urchin who has just let a rattlesnake out of a bunny-sack and is wondering why he did it.

For his part, Mudcat sat a moment massaging his forearms and hands. When he could flex his fingers, he rolled to his knees behind the snoring Ira Shank and whispered savagely to the wide-eyed boy, "Gimme the knife, kid—!"

The meaning and the motion of this tableau was now clear even to an eight-year-old sod-house boy. There was murder in the stillness of his father's stock shed, and the Shuffman lad drew back and felt the fear of Mudcat Clevenger's wild stare drive into him. The Missourian sensed this change, and knew that the next instant could still wreck his thin chance to stay alive. With a muffled curse he came to his feet and started for the boy.

But only started.

The child uttered a gasp of terror and cried out, "No! don't hurt me!" and behind Mudcat's bent form Ira Shank muttered something and came groggily to one elbow, peering about in the still half-darkened gloom of the shed to determine what had awakened him. He never found out. Clevenger whirled about, seized up the broken whiffletree from the floor of the first stall, and drove its iron tug-eyed end into the back of the Kansan's head.

Shank made no sound and Mudcat knew that he never would. But the delay had cost him something he could not afford—the sod-house boy.

He was gone. He seemed to have vanished into the musty air of the shed. Yet he had not run out the open front, nor had he passed Mudcat and Shank to reach

96

the wagon stall. He was back under the hay. He had to be.

But when Mudcat had thrown aside the last bundle he, as Schlonager and Scortini after him, found nothing but the hard rammed earth of the shed's floor.

Then he saw the oat bin.

12

SCHLONAGER LAY ON THE OPPOSITE BANK WATCHING the wolf hole under the lip of the low bluff across from him. No sound or motion came from the hole. It had been an hour since he and Scortini had found Shank dead. For half of that time Schlonager had lain on his stomach thirty feet from the hole glaring at it. No thought had come to him on how he might get at Mudcat Clevenger without threat to the sod-house woman and her children. He did not know, even, if they were still alive, or if, in his varmint's wildness, Mudcat had killed them. He did not think the latter would be the case, however. It was obvious to a sane person that Mrs. Shuffman and those three kids would be hard to beat for hostage. But how sane was Mudcat?

Schlonager didn't know that either. He didn't know anything, really, except that he had come here to find that woman and those three kids and he was going to find them. Then he was going to take them back to Fort Pitchfork, as his orders from Captain Hobart had read.

He ground his blunt teeth together, hating what he had to do now, yet not daring further delay.

"Clevenger," he called across the creek, "what's your deal? What do you want of us out here?"

His first reply was silence, and the terrible fear arose that Mudcat had harmed his companions. But presently the Missourian called back.

"I been thinking about that," he said.

Schlonager nodded. "Keep thinking about it," he said. "Mrs. Shuffman? Are you and the kids all right in there?"

Again there was the stretching, soundless wait, and again the crawling, nameless fear. Then the woman's voice came, muffled but clear and steady, from the den's passage. "Yes, we're all right. Who are you out there?"

"Soldiers from Fort Pitchfork," said Schlonager. "I'm Sergeant Schlonager. We're here to pick up you and the kids. We found out from your husband where you were—I mean here at Gooseberry Crossing. Now, don't worry, Ma'am. We're going to get you out of there. Just don't be jumpy or foolish. Do what Clevenger says."

"Is my husband dead?" the woman asked.

Damn that Clevenger, thought Schlonager. He had told her. That was a purely vicious thing to do. No need for that whatever. Except to be wicked.

"Yes," he said, "the Sioux got him, Ma'am. We gave him decent burial. His last words were for you and the kids. Clevenger—"

"Yeah?"

"What's your deal?"

He heard the rough chuckle and the curse from the wolf den. Then Mudcat called sharply, "I got a beauty for you; listen to this." He held up, letting the seconds drag, savoring his enemy's torment. "Soon as it's dark," he said, "you have my saddled horse led into the shed up yonder. Me and the woman and these yawpy brats will come up through the oat bin, with me last and holding onto the baby for insurance. You see that part of it good and plain, you big dumb ox?"

"You will have the baby," Schlonager repeated carefully, "so that we won't jump you or try anything funny, for fear of getting it hurt. Is that right?"

"That's exactly right. And you know I'd hurt it, too, don't you, Schlonager?"

"Go on," said the big sergeant. "What else?"

"I'll take my horse and the baby and ride out down the river toward Greybull. I ought to be able to make the settlement by daybreak. It's a good trail and I know it by heart."

"So do the Sioux," said Schlonager. "What about them?"

"They're your problem, Sergeant. Ain't you the famous Indian lover and expert? Ain't you the great Sergeant Schlonager, the friend of the noble red man and oldest regular army sergeant west of Laramie or Fort Lincoln?"

"You mean I'm to create a diversion while you get away down the river?"

"Yeah, and it better be a good one. That is, if Mrs. Shuffman here wants to see her kid in good shape again. It's a girl, Schlonager. You know how tickled them Sioux are to get white baby girls."

"Keep your damned mouth shut," said Schlonager. "At least do that."

"Sure, sure," laughed the other. "You just remember I'll have that kid. You do that, and I'll leave her in Greybull with those folks that run the store. I reckon me and the baby will be the only survivors of this here surround, Schlonager. That's the part gives me the positive pleasures."

"Clevenger, just be careful with the woman and those kids. You know me. You know I mean what I say. I'll tear your—never mind, just be cautious and move slow. We'll do the same."

"I know you will. Now about that deal; we got it understood, or ain't we?"

"I'll have to talk with Scortini and the others."

"The hell you will. They'll do what you say. So what do you say?"

"You heard what I said," announced Schlonager, getting up and scanning the ground between himself and the shed. "I'll be back. But I want to see them kids before I go. Mrs. Shuffman, what's their names?"

"Marybell is the girl; she's fourteen. Huffaker's the boy; he's eight and a half, going on nine."

"Clevenger, let the girl show her face in the cliff hole. Easy now."

He heard the scuffle of movement in the den, then saw the wan face peering at him from the bank-side gloom of the den entrance. It was a pretty face, and not frightened. "You all right, honey?" asked Schlonager. The girl nodded. "Yes, sir," she said, "we're right fine. It's a good hole, and the soldier ain't hurt us."

"Clevenger, show the boy."

The lad came into view grinning. He was dirty and tousled and tear-stained but that was only natural from what had gone before. Now he was getting his second wind and enjoying being held hostage in a wolf's den by a "rennygade" cavalry soldier. "How do, Sergeant," he called out. "You going to fight this other feller in here? Looks to me like you could whip him easy as pie. You got any kids? Little boys like me, or big girls like Marybell?"

"No," said Schlonager, "I haven't got anything, not even good sense. What do they call you? Huff?"

"Yes, sir. That's what my dad calls me. Maw says Huffaker, but that there's her maiden name and she's right determined to call me by the full thing. Huff's what the men call me. What's your name?"

"Honus," said Schlonager. "Kind of goes good with Huff, don't it?"

"Goes fine," said the little boy. "When you going to get us out of the hole? You ain't acherally going to let this rennygade take the baby, be you? Baby ain't too lively, you know. Been puny since spring. That's where Paw went, to fetch medicine."

"Huff," said the sergeant, "you look out for your Maw and your sisters, you hear? Do what Clevenger says."

"You mean old Mudcat? I ain't afraid of him now that you're here. I can see that he ain't no match for you. You'll whup him 'thout half trying."

"Shut up, boy!" warned Schlonager quickly. "You do what he says and don't talk smart, you hear me?"

"Sure, yes sir, all right. Hurry up, will you? I want to see them Injuns when they come a'helling back to fight your soldiers. That ought to be just great. I ain't never see'd a first-class Injun fight."

"Be quiet," said Schlonager, "and do what you're told."

He set off across the clearing, after sweeping both north and south ridges to be sure no Sioux sat upon them. What the devil was he going to do now? He couldn't let that crazy Clevenger take that baby and ride out with her. The heartless fiend would just as soon throw her in the Big Horn or bash her little head against a pine trunk the first turn of the trail downstream. He was that kind. Killing didn't register in his brain as it did in the brains of normal men. It didn't mean anything to Mudcat. It wasn't even as much of a decision for him as would be shooting a good dog, or a stout horse. He was one of those human monsters who had built himself into such a position within himself that to take another person's life was no more important to him than to take that person's pocketbook, and maybe somewhat less profitable. That was just the trouble. He knew this about Mudcat Clevenger. Scortini might suspect it, or he might not. The others would hate Clevenger but would not realize that he was literally a crazed man. They wouldn't be able to weigh that fact on the scales by which they replied to Schlonager's report of the Missourian's "deal." And they also had their own lives to think of first. Mudcat's deal, whatever its terms, certainly did nothing to increase the odds of these soldiers getting back to Fort Pitchfork. It was a hard choice. Perhaps there might be an alternative to it. Maybe the men would think of some third course not apparent to Schlonager. There had to be *some* way.

He was halfway to the house, plodding head down and scowling, when the Sioux rifles began to crack from the south ridge, and the lead to whine and spang off the baked earth and rocks of the clearing about him.

13

AS HE RAN, SCHLONAGER KNEW A SUDDEN DREAD. THE Sioux were not shooting at him. It was the horses. They had come down the ridge to positions where they could shoot into the picket line, and the Fort Pitchfork horses were grunting and going down like slaughter beeves even as he sprinted cursingly in among them.

By this time, Squint and Harry Albion were around the corner of the cabin and firing back into the rocks above. A moment later, Pulaski came stumbling up and joined in the return fire. The effect was to diminish the Indian attack, as the red riflemen, although well protected by rock and scrub, had no stomach for holding an aimed shot under a hail of U.S. lead. As their Winchesters and old Springfields subsided, Squint dashed in among the mounts with Schlonager. In seconds they had the surviving animals cut loose and dragged around the far wall of the cabin and through its low door, into the cramped interior. But the damage had been done. Six horses were down on the line. Of the five Schlonager and Squint had been able to get inside, all were hit superficially. They might or might not be serviceable. There was no attempt on Schlonager's part to either minimize or disclaim responsibility for the tragedy.

"I knew," he said in the silence that followed the entrance of the last horse and man into the Shuffman cabin, "that we ought to have put them down in the shed."

Scortini, who had been left in the shed to watch the oat-bin exit of the wolf hole, and who had left his post to run up to the sod house under the Indian fire, now growled a Sicilian obscenity, and denied the allegation.

"The hell!" he said. "We talked it over last night and we both decided they'd be safe picketed out back. Besides, the damned shed wouldn't hold but five of them and you saved five. So where's your fault in that arithmetic?"

"We could have put them all under roof," said Schlonager. "We talked of that too. Five in the shed, and six in here. Remember?"

"I do," said Squint Hibbard. "We always used to fort-up the horses when the Comanches were out. That's down home to West Texas, I mean. No criticism, Sergeant."

Schlonager accepted it.

"We were tired," he said. "We were all so tired and rode out and stupid with fatigue we none of us knew enough to dig in as we ought to have. But the fault is mine. If you don't think so, ask Captain Hobart when we get back."

"That's the second time you've made that joke about getting back," said Scortini. "This time I ain't laughing at it, though. Somehow, it don't strike me uproarious."

Private Harry Albion nodded his skeletal head. "I find myself also able to restrain the more vulgar risibilities," he said. "I think a polite grin is all I can spare at the moment. No offense, Sergeant Schlonager."

Pulaski, even, was constrained to comment, and perhaps with more blunt accuracy than his more intelligent fellows. "No joke," he mumbled. "Damn. Bad as hell."

Scortini reached over and patted him on the top of the head, as though he were a dog that had just fetched the paper without tearing it up. "Good boy, good boy," he said. "Now go over and lie down and shut up."

"Well," said Schlonager, when the silence had returned, "if that didn't bring a laugh, perhaps this will." He proceeded to tell them of the murder of Ira Shank and the holing-up of the crazed killer with Mrs. Shuffman and the three children in the wolf den under the bank of the creek. "Now then," he shrugged, finishing the grim report, "if that doesn't tickle your funny bones, then nothing will."

"My God," breathed Squint Hibbard, "that wild dog has got them poor little kids and that brave sweet woman cornered in a damn wolf hole? I cain't believe it. How'd he get loose? I tied them knots myself!"

"I know you did," said Schlonager, "but the knot hasn't been invented that can't be untied with a knife. Somebody either cut him loose, or he was able to saw them apart on something sharp, which he took with him. Scortini and me couldn't figure it out."

"Another thing," suggested Harry Albion, drawing on his pipe and pointing with its stem to make his idea emphatic, "if the bottom of the oat bin was a hinged trap door, swinging downward as you say, why would it not have been clean of oat and corn debris when you and Scortini first looked at it last night? The woman and the kids would have used it to get into the hole, according to your thinking, and if they had, would that use not have 'cleaned the boards' so to speak, as did Clevenger's subsequent use of it?"

Schlonager and Scortini stared at one another. The corporal recovered first.

"Chalk up another demerit to too much work and not enough time off," he said. "We must have been as dumb for lack of sleep, both of us, as I accused you of being by your lonesome," he said to the huge German. "I never gave that part of it a thought, did you?"

"No," replied Schlonager, "I never did."

"It's true, though," said Squint. "It's got to be."

"Yes, it has," admitted Schlonager.

A third stillness settled on the packed room, while the men again thought of their circumstances. It was a terrible thing about that poor woman and her kids, but how about their own wolf hole? This damned filthy sod-house trap in which they were buried as surely and even a lot less comfortably than the people under the creek bank? How about that? Weighing Mudcat Clevenger against the angry Sioux out there on the ridge—two dozen of them Schlonager had said—it did not seem that Mrs. Shuffman and the children were any worse off than they were. In fact, the Shuffman chances of escaping the Indians were better with Mudcat and the wolf hole, than were their own chances with Schlonager and the sod-house cabin. It was Harry Albion, the pipe smoker and thinker of the detail, who pointed this out.

"I would estimate," the Englishman said, "that Mrs. Shuffman and the youngsters are safer where they are than if with us. I don't quite see what we have to offer them by 'rescuing' them. Rescuing them *from* what, *for* what? Personally, Sergeant, were I to have the similar choice, I am morally certain I should prefer to gamble with Mudcat than with those bloody red men. Am I not correct?"

Schlonager, on guard at the open door, did not reply. Instead, he called to Scortini, at the rear-wall rifle slit.

"You see anything on your side?"

"No," said the corporal, "not a thing. How about you?"

"Nothing," answered Schlonager. "That was a picked bunch sent over to get the horses. The others will still be camped behind that north ridge most likely."

"Yeah," agreed Scortini, "I guess. I can see breakfast-fire smoke over there. Wispy and faint, but smoke for sure."

"Sergeant," said Harry Albion, "did you hear my query?"

"Yes, I heard it." Schlonager didn't turn from his watch post at the door. "It doesn't do you proud, Harry."

"Perhaps not, but how about its logic—its sense?"

"Sound, I reckon. If you want only to think of making sense. There's more to it than that, I think."

The Englishman drew on his pipe. He exhaled with a slow nod, as though he could agree to the possibility, but his companion, Squint Hibbard, could not see it.

"Such as what, Sergeant?" frowned the cowboy road agent. "Seems to me that Harry's hit it square-on. Left in the hole with Mudcat, the lady and the kids got a far better chance than if we dig them out. You seriously argue that?"

"Yes. What makes sense isn't always what's right."

"How's that?"

"You know what I mean, Squint; many times a man talks himself into doing what's the easiest for him by telling himself that it's the 'sensible' thing to do. In my life, I've done it plenty. I'm not going to do it here."

The Texas cowboy's lean face was hardening. Behind him, tall Harry Albion and scowling Casimir Pulaski watched Schlonager with narrowed eyes. Even Scortini took his gaze from the rifle slit and fastened it on the sergeant.

"Why not?" demanded Squint.

"Because," said Schlonager, "I've got my orders. They say to find this woman and her kids and bring them back to the fort. We've found them, and we will bring them back."

"Just like that, eh?" said Harry Albion. "Bloody big of you, I'd say, Sergeant. But rather embarrassing."

"Oh? In what way, Harry?"

"We may as well be candid, Sergeant; we face a delicate situation, here. We all want to live. We have five horses which seem to be substantially fit. There are five of us. Also substantially fit. I am sure the same thought has occurred to Scortini and Squint, and I would not wonder greatly that it had filtered even into the dim and unlit recesses of that cranial coal pit which is the intellect of Private Pulaski; and the thought is this: if we five were to ride out of here tonight, rested and determined, the odds are better than even that we would elude the Sioux entirely, or, at very worst, get a good start upon them and be well home before they might come up to us in pursuit. I believe that when one considers the likelihood of Captain Hobart having dispatched a search patrol when we do not return on schedule this evening, and the attendant likelihood of that patrol encountering us before the Sioux can do the same—well, Sergeant, I am sure that this is logic and also that it is right. What do you say, sir? Will you contest us?"

Schlonager put his head down and frowned hard for thirty seconds. Even Scortini, who knew him best, was not sure if he were seeking to control his temper or merely to marshal his reasonable arguments. Finally, he looked up.

"What do you mean, will I 'contest' you?" he asked.

The Englishman colored, stammering a little. "You make it bloody difficult, old man," he said. "I don't like to spell it out. Especially when there is no real need."

"There's a real need," said Schlonager. "Start spelling."

Harry Albion now found it his turn to put his head down. He could not face Schlonager and say what was on his tongue. And he was too much the gentleman to say it without facing him. So he looked down and said nothing.

"I know," said Schlonager slowly, and letting his blue eyes study the rest of them, "what Harry meant. So does each man of you. But he didn't say it, and it won't go in the record. Unless you want it to."

Mario Scortini, the nominal second-in-command of the decimated patrol, stepped away from his rifle slit. His glittering, hard, black eyes caught Schlonager's. "Harry's right, you know, Honus. You're making it tough as hell for the rest of us. You're pushing us over the edge."

Schlonager looked at him unwaveringly.

"You are a damned liar, Mario," he said. "You're pushing yourselves over the edge."

"By God, sir!" exclaimed Harry Albion, "I don't see it! Scortini is right. You're making those orders an obsession. You've been wrong since we left the fort, or at least since we were ambushed in Cottonwood Rocks. I must tell you, sir, that no commander in his right mind would have gone on past that point in view of the situation we faced. For a non-commissioned officer to take it upon himself to expose this patrol in the manner you have done, would be grounds for a military trial in any army in the civilized world. You propose to try Clevenger for murder, Sergeant; what do you suppose would be the nature of the indictment for yourself?"

"What would have happened to the woman and the kids if we hadn't come on past Cottonwood Rocks?" asked Schlonager quietly.

"What's going to happen to them now that we

111

have?" demanded the Englishman. "Indeed, they may have had a better chance without us poking around to lead the Sioux to remain here. They may have seen you and Scortini down there this morning, and be wondering what interests you at the creek. Did you ever think of that, Sergeant?"

"Yes, I hid myself down there. And I kept my voice down."

"But they could have seen you?"

"Yes."

"And been made suspicious?"

"I doubt that. They don't think like we do. Besides, there was no other way. I couldn't let Clevenger sit down there with those people all day, could I? Put yourself in the woman's place. Remember the baby. Apparently, it's only a small one, still on milk. And the older girl, she's fourteen. That's nearly grown. That's really two women under there with that mad dog."

"We didn't know that; we thought they were all little kids. Come on, Honus, be fair. We ain't trying to do anything but what's best for all. That includes those poor people in the wolf hole. Even Mudcat."

It was Scortini, taking over for Harry Albion, and Schlonager knew that the corporal meant what he said and was not thinking altogether of his own skin.

"All right," he said, "what will happen if we take the five horses and ride out of here tonight?"

"You mean to the woman and kids?"

"Sure."

"Well, we'll send back a column to pick them up. You know Captain Hobart. He'll do it. Why the hell you think he sent Lieutenant Gilliam out in the first place? It was the damned woman. Her and the kids. Little kids, like we all thought. And a good woman. Well?"

"You're right about Hobart. You're wrong about sending back a column. What if we don't make it to the fort?"

"Don't make it? Hell, you're the one been insisting all along that we would. We'll make it, all right. We will if we ride out tonight, the five of us, and keep going hard all night."

"But if we didn't make it?" persisted Schlonager. "If we rode out tonight and the Sioux got to us between here and Pitchfork, then what?"

"You mean about the woman and kids?"

"You know what I mean, Mario."

"Well, hell, they wouldn't be no worse off. Fact is, we would have drawn the Sioux away from them, and they could go on down the river to Greybull. They're frontier folks. They could do it. It ain't like they were wagon-train settlers, not used to the country."

"And what about Mudcat? What about leaving him with that woman and that young girl? I haven't seen the woman but the girl is pretty. And well grown."

"My God!" exploded Scortini. "We can't cover everything, Honus. We're talking about saving our lives, not some sod-house woman's pride, or her kid's virtue! Be reasonable!"

"I'm trying," said Honus Schlonager wearily. "It's not easy."

"It never is, my dear sir," said Harry Albion. "You don't suppose it has been, or is easy, for us to suggest leaving that poor thing and her children under that bank with a dog like Mudcat Clevenger? Come, now, Sergeant, I'm sure you know us all better than that!"

"I'm not sure," said Schlonager, "that I know anything about any of you. And I'm *certain* that you haven't learned much about me. Not you, Harry. Not you, Squint. Not you, Mario, not even you . . ."

The omitting of Pulaski was not unnoticed. It was Albion, again, who called the question. In response, Schlonager only shrugged, and said, "I don't know about Pulaski; he may be thinking the same as me: he hasn't said."

The three soldiers fell silent, studying the scowling Pole. It was Squint Hibbard who turned to Schlonager and drawled sarcastically, "Why don't you ask him?"

"I would," said the hulking German sergeant, "but I don't know what to ask him."

Harry Albion nodded his slightly superior British nod. Mario Scortini grinned too, a dry, cowboy grin, that said much and hinted a great deal more. For his slow, untutored part, Casimir Pulaski looked neither pleased, nor crafty, nor superior. His ugly face and bent body seemed only to grow more resentful, more resistant, to the company of his fellows and the commands of his sergeant. They were all watching him now, and they thought they could see him retreating farther and farther inward into the bitter shell of hostility and defense that his evil reputation had built around him. But they were wrong. The Pole was not retreating, and he was not confused.

He walked over to Schlonager's side and stood facing the hard-breathing, sweat-streaked figures of his comrades and his self-appointed betters. Just for a moment he seemed to stand straight and to show a gleam of some other, inside light, through the black glower of his scowl.

"Damn to hell," he rumbled in his deep voice, "we will get that woman and those kids out of there."

Schlonager put his arm about the sloping shoulders and stood there feeling strong and sure and renewed.

"You're right, Pulaski," he said, "we will."

14

"HOLD THE HOUSE AND THE HORSES," SAID SCHLONAGER, and Scortini nodded and answered, "Sure," then added cynically, "how long?"

Schlonager held up in the doorway. "If we're not back in—" he paused and said, "What time is it now?"

The corporal grinned and dug out his watch. "Seven," he said. "And that's important."

"How come?"

"Why, time is one of the things that separates us from the animals," replied Scortini, straight-faced. "You got to keep track of the time."

Schlonager stared at him. "That's right," he said, "I'd forgot."

"You've been busy," nodded the corporal. "It's only natural. Well, how long you want us to wait?"

"If we're not back by ten, you're on your own."

"Three hours till it's legal to cut and run, eh?"

"You won't run, Mario. It's too much work."

"True, true; but the first law of my tribe is to survive."

"The first law of your tribe is to avoid honest work."

"The hell! You're just not cultured enough to appreciate a fine Sicilian gentleman when you meet one."

"Maybe not. I'll be better able to tell after I've met one. Watch sharp for the Sioux. Come on, Pulaski."

He and the Pole went outside and slid along the front wall of the cabin and around its front corner into the open meadow of the clearing. They moved as though they were walking on broken glass in their bare feet the first few steps, but no Indian fire greeted them. They grinned at each other, Schlonager first and then Pulaski imitating him awkwardly. They went the rest of the way to the shed at an unhurried walk, this, so that if the Sioux were observing from a distance, they would not be aroused to investigate more closely. After all, what was suspicious about a sergeant and one of his troopers going down to the stock shed of the dead white man, Shuffman, the one armed only with a shovel and the other with the settler woman's stove-wood ax? At the shed, ducking just inside its open front and after quickly checking the oat bin to see that it was closed, Schlonager and his soldier held a briefing.

"All right, Pulaski, let's go over it once more."

He held up his hand and ticked off the points of the operation, bending down one thick finger for each point. The Pole stood watching the fingers and nodding and licking his lips as each digit was folded over. When he had finished, Schlonager said, "Now, you sure you want to try it? You got a good argument and I know you don't lack the will, but I don't know about letting you do it; it don't seem right."

The Pole frowned. His ugly face furrowed itself, the blond, thick brows knitting and bristling like the hair of an angry dog's back. He struggled for the words.

"It's right," he managed finally. "God tells me so."

Schlonager nodded, frowning in turn.

In a sense, it *was* right, he knew. Pulaski had argued for the dangerous half of the attempt on the basis of his experience as a coal miner. This was no idle claim to the honor of the greater risk, for those years of working on his belly with eighteen inches overhead and six on either side and still being able to swing a short pick, to move, to go forward or backward, even to double and turn in spaces where the inexperienced could not even breathe without becoming panic-stricken, all this could not be discounted. Not when your goal was a helpless woman and three children held captive by a madman. Not when the very first swing of the pick—or the hand ax—had to be the only one. Not where the least sound of approach or hint of carelessly scraped dirt falling from side or top of the tunnel, might send the desperate Clevenger into a spasm of viciousness. Wherever he was crouched with those poor people in the dark channel of the wolf den, his carbine and the knife which had freed him would be but inches from the four innocent victims of his demented break for freedom.

The Pole, studying Schlonager's face as these thoughts toiled in the sergeant's mind, suddenly reached out and put his hand diffidently on Schlonager's arm.

"The eyes," he muttered, "don't forget the eyes."

He pointed with a grimy forefinger, as he spoke, to his own starey, light-colored and peculiarly piercing orbs.

Like a mine mule, he had told Schlonager, the eyes of the man who worked the midnight pits of the Pennsylvania fields became different. They became so that the man could see in the dark. Could see and feel his way, too, in a manner no surface fellow could achieve. Eventually, like the mule, he went blind. But before that time there was a time of unusual keenness of vision underground. And Pulaski had said that he had this vision, he knew that he had, and that it would let him do the "inside" part of the plan better than any man, even than Schlonager.

Now, as the squat Pole stood with his fingers moving slowly from one to the other of his eyes and nodding his shaggy, misshapen head at his companion, Schlonager made his final decision.

"All right," he said, with the small stiff twist of the wide lips which, with him, passed for a smile, "the 'eyes' have it."

It was a very tiny joke and surely Casimir Pulaski never understood it, but he returned the smile as though he had, and, moreover, as though he had appreciated the entire nature of the agreement.

"By damn," he said, "it's good with me and you."

Schlonager, turning to leave the shed, paused, the shovel hanging at his side. "Pulaski," he said, "I still can't figure it out. What's in it for you? Is it the woman?" He watched the Pole closely when he said it, and did not miss the expression of anguish that crossed the other's coarse features. He waited, nonetheless, sensing that Pulaski wanted to answer him.

"Yes," said the latter finally, "the woman."

"But not this woman, is that it?"

"No, the other one."

"Your wife, Pulaski?"

The Pole looked at him, reaching out his gnarled hands in mute silence, then dropping his shoulders and saying stolidly, "Yes, the wife . . . I do it for her."

"You loved your wife," said Schlonager. "Very much, I think."

Pulaski raised his head. He studied his companion's face, seeming to seek and ask for the truth of the words. Schlonager, feeling this, nodded imperceptibly. The Pole returned the slight motion and said softly, "Thank you . . ."

With that, he turned away and padded cautiously across the dirt floor of the shed to his post by the closed and musty oat-bin entrance of the wolf-hole escape tunnel. The last Schlonager saw of him, he was standing looking down at the silent bin, his blunt fingers opening and closing with relentless, reflex force on the worn haft of Mrs. Shuffman's stove-wood hand ax.

15

THE CENTRAL ROOM OF THE PASSAGEWAY WAS PERHAPS six by eight feet in area, with a three-foot ceiling. This was the denning room of the wolf hole under the creek bank. From it, the tunnel led seven feet to the bank and some thirty twisting feet to the oat bin in the stock shed. It made a commodious hiding place, even for four humans and a human beast. Scanning it now by the guttering light of the antelope-tallow candle, Mudcat Clevenger had no reason to hide his vacant grin of pleasure. It would take some brains and brawn greater than those of that stupid Dutchman to beat these diggings. It seemed to Mudcat that, finally, an unfair fate had dealt him a hand of cards he could play to the last pile of chips. It was a good feeling.

Beneath its glow, Mudcat expanded.

"If you all stay quiet and mind what I tell you," he said to the Shuffmans, "this thing here will work out all right, and with nobody hurt." He leered at Mrs.

Shuffman, and added, "Course, that depends on how easy some of you hurt. Eh, Ma'am?"

The woman was careful with him. She had long ago sensed that they were dealing with a deranged mind, if not a depraved man. She was not a fool, this Mrs. Dulcie Shuffman. She may have been, once, when she married Abel Shuffman, and she may have been, twice, when she agreed to come to Wyoming with him, and, three times, when she had let him talk her into sneaking into this posted basin and trying to homestead. But, no, not even then had she really been a fool. She had known what must happen and had only failed to know how to prevent Abel Shuffman from making it happen. Now, with Shuffman gone, and trapped here with her children with still some slim chance to come out all right, Dulcie Shuffman was not going to let pride and decency and properness infringe on that chance. She did not smile at Mudcat, nor encourage him, but she did answer him.

"We meant to do what you say, Mr. Clevenger," she told him. "We've no reason to want ill to come to you."

"I have," put in little Huff. "He stoled my knife."

"Be quiet, Huff. Speak when you're spoke to."

"But Paw give me that knife. It was a genoowine Green River. Stamped right on the blade, and everything."

Mudcat reached out and hit him with the back of his hand. It was not a wicked blow, but it sent the youth sprawling. "Do what your Maw says," he warned quietly.

121

"That's right," said Dulcie Shuffman quickly.

At her words, Mudcat spread his rotten-toothed grin. "You see," he said to the older girl, Marybell, who sat staring at him with unmasked revulsion, "there ain't nobody going to get hurt long as they do what your Maw and Mudcat say. No sir, no sir . . ." He let the words trail away, his attitude suddenly tensing.

"Somebody's outside!" he rasped. "Don't none of you move or I'll shoot you." He held the cocked carbine on the group, wriggling toward the creek-bank entrance and shouting angrily, "What's out there? Speak up, damn you, or I'll shoot me a kid!"

"It's only me, Clevenger," answered Schlonager. "I've come back from the boys. They say your deal's good."

"By God, they better. Now you get out of here and stay away till dusk, you hear me?"

Schlonager stuck the head of the shovel into the hole opening. "You see this?" he said.

"You're crazy!" snarled the Missourian. "You start digging in here with that, I'll kill every one of these brats, and the woman, too!"

"I'm not going to dig in to get at you," said Schlonager, "but I've got to fill in this end of the tunnel. Now, you look out here a minute and I'll show you what I mean."

"You *are* crazy!" raged Mudcat. "I stick my head out and one of your heroes knocks it off with a carbine butt! I warned you, Schlonager. You fool around with me and—"

"Nobody's fooling around," said Schlonager. "You don't have to stick your head out of the hole to see what I want you to see. Just look across the creek. You can see that south sky, can't you? There above the ridge?"

"Yeah."

"What do you see?"

"Black cloud roiling. Heat lightning. Gonna rain like hell. That don't bother me none. What's your point?"

"She comes on to cloudburst, as she looks to threaten," answered Schlonager, "this dinky creek will be up that bank in twenty minutes. We're powerful close to two big ridges and the drainage from the river bluff. Listen to that thunder roll, Clevenger. You know weather sign in this country by now. Inside half an hour hell won't hold the water that'll be coming down this creek."

"You're a damned fool!" shouted the other. "You don't get around me with that blind dodge. You think old wolf he gonna dig a hole that'll flood when the creek comes up?"

"Old wolf," said Schlonager slowly and mimickingly, "he don't dig this hole for times when the water's up. Old wolf he dig this hole for the winter. Creek's froze solid all the while old wolf raising his family in there. You hear that thunder, Clevenger. She's coming over this prairie on the gallop!"

"But air?" cried the renegade soldier, "what we gonna do for air? If you seal up the creek-side hole, there won't be no draft working!"

The thunder and heavy lightning had begun splitting the sky immediately behind the south ridge, and as Clevenger watched from the narrow hole, the gray sheet of the rain began to move over the ridge and advance down its dusty flanks toward the creek. He could hear the hollow drum of its power on the baked earth, and he knew it was no ordinary summer shower but a real prairie storm, what was locally called a gully-washer and a channel-straightener.

"Don't worry about the air," called Schlonager. "We will open the oat bin for you. That'll give you all you need till tonight. What do you say, now? I don't worry about you, you know that. But it's wrong to let this water in on the others. Ask Mrs. Shuffman if it gets into the tunnel during a hard summer rain. Maybe I'm wrong. I sure don't want to do anything wrong."

"Dig, damn you!" yelled Mudcat, backing away from the rain driving into the mouth of the hole. "Plug her tight but just remember that the first funny move from the other end and—"

The first rattling shovelful hit into the tunnel mouth, cutting off his words. Another followed and another. The gray aperture of sheeting rain narrowed to nothing and was gone. Beyond the sealed entrance they could still hear the thud and chug of Schlonager's shovel forcing and tamping the bank clay into the opening. The candle, which had been burning steadily in the draft of pure air now cut off by the closure, flickered violently, went down, nearly dying. Mudcat cried out a vile string of curses and writhed into the denning room from the outer tunnel. "Somebody's coming!" he hissed. "That damned Schlonager was talking me off. He was keeping me listening, while they came in the other end. That candle jumped like hell just now!" He slid past Dulcie and the children, lips twisting, eyes wild. The sod-house woman called after him, low voiced. "Sure the flame jumped, Mr. Clevenger. That was from the draft being cut off by the sergeant plugging the hole yonder. Now you see it's steadied up again. Look—"

There was desperation in her tones, for she did not know if the madman spoke the truth, and if help, indeed, might be coming down that low corridor from the oat bin. Something of her intensity caught at Clevenger. He paused, looking back. The candle had steadied. It was burning calmly as before. He hesitated, not really certain of too much now. He knew that he had lost something of his advantage to the hated sergeant. Schlonager had outwitted him in some way. Of that he was positive. Yet there could be no doubt, either, of that storm coming on out there. The argument about the denning season of the wolves was also solid. But there was still something wrong with all this, and very badly wrong with it.

"Hesh up!" he warned the woman. "All of you hesh up. Hold even your breathing. I want to listen."

Dulcie Shuffman gestured to her children to obey. They nodded and were still. She clutched the baby more closely to her breast, but it gave a thin cry which seemed to tear at the deepening silence. Clevenger whirled, eyes blazing.

"Keep that whelp quiet!" he raged, "or I'll smash her head in." He crawled back to the woman with the threat, crouching above her, the carbine butt poised menacingly.

Dulcie Shuffman pressed against the den wall, terror at last rising in her voice. "My God, please, please—"

In her natural human fear she could not think, but in his unnatural animal ugliness, Mudcat Clevenger could. He seized her blouse, ripping it away from her full breasts.

"Feed the kid, damn you!" he mumbled, staring at her pantingly. "You got more'n enough there!"

She twisted away, turning her white shoulder to his hot gaze, giving the baby to nurse in such a sheltered way as not to excite further the gaunt, wild-eyed trooper.

But Clevenger's breathing grew thicker and he made no motion to return to the candle that he had picked up and set out of the way upon the cavern floor behind him by the mouth of the tunnel leading to the oat bin. Dulcie Shuffman knew, then, that she could not face the moment with this man. Naked fear crowded in, forcing out reason. She opened her mouth for the scream that would signal the onset of irreversible hysteria. But the sound never issued. In the last instant before its birth, her frozen gaze had seen something move in the gaping bowel of the tunnel behind Clevenger, and her lips closed and her voice, when it came, was strangely low and certain.

"Wait," she murmured to the lurching Mudcat, "It's not right for the children." She held forth the baby to her white-faced older daughter. "Take the little one, Marybell," she ordered. "You and Huff go up and lay in the bank hole. Wait there till I call you back. You understand this, Marybell?"

The girl nodded miserably, fighting for control of her nerves and her words.

"Yes, Maw," she said. "I'm most growed . . ."

When the children had gone and when they lay with their feet toward the denning room, quietly in the outer tunnel, Dulcie Shuffman turned to the hovering Clevenger and reaching her soft bare arms toward him. He made a wordless noise in his throat, neither human nor sane, and bent forward.

As he did, an arm, thick and merciless and heavily muscled as the strangling coil of a python, came out of the mine-shaft blackness of the far tunnel. Its poised hand hovered an instant over the small clear flame of the candle on the floor, then closed soundlessly upon it.

The blindness of the stygian pit rushed inward upon the denning room.

16

CLEVENGER STRAIGHTENED AND TWISTED ABOUT. HE struck his head ringingly against the low ceiling and grunted in pain. His first thought was for his carbine. Intuitively, he reached for it. He didn't think about it, he just reached. After all, he knew where it was; knew where he had put it aside only the moment before. His hand closed only upon the sand of the den floor. Reacting with a fright almost of its own, the hand switched this way and that, groping, grasping, plunging into the empty sand. Nothing. It felt nothing. The carbine was gone.

He hesitated, his mind knowing that whirling lostness which comes with the sense of being disoriented in total darkness. As long as he had believed he knew where he was, and where things were in relationship to him, there had been no fear in him. He had a gun and whoever had come after him down the oat-bin tunnel could not have anything better than a gun. He didn't ask more than that. He could feel and fight in the dark as well as any man he had ever encountered. It was a part of his guerrilla training and experience. But now. Now that the gun was not where he had thought it was . . . a second thought came upon him. Perhaps he had *not* lost his sense of direction in whirling about to face the candle snuffer. Maybe he *had* known where the gun was, and maybe the gun was no longer there. Frantically, he swept his long arms in a full circle about him. His reach, he knew, must enclose the area in which he had put down the Spencer Carbine. Yet his taloned fingers struck nothing save the soft calf and ankle of the Shuffman woman. The gun *was* gone.

Again, Clevenger forced himself to hold still and to think. The knife! That was it. He still had the kid's knife and he still had the kid's mother. He would put the two together and dare his enemy to move against him at the price of the blade going into the woman's stomach. In the same swift motion, he unsheathed the knife and circled his long left arm outward through the darkness to gather in Dulcie Shuffman. The arm, as the hand groping for the gun before it, closed on the empty blackness. The woman, probably alerted and galvanized by the touch of his searching hand the moment before, had moved away from him. She, too, was gone!

But wait now. She could not have gotten far. Most likely she had only slid backward and gone into the outer creek-bank hole with her kids. He had only to feel straight ahead until he came to the hole, and there she would be. Grinning, Mudcat Clevenger eased forward through the dark. Again he knew quick frustration. His feeling hand struck the hard clay of the den's wall. He moved it right and left. Still only the wall. No hole. No soft white leg. No hostage to buy his life and liberty. Nothing. Not a sight or a sound or a shuffle of movement in that shroud of black hell. "*Damn you!*" screamed Mudcat, "I'll get you! I've got a knife, I've got a knife . . ."

129

His answer was utter stillness.

He waited, breathing shallowly, trying to hear.

Off to his right, a rattle of sand, dry and scraping, came faintly. He leaped in the direction. The force with which he crashed into the hardpan clay of the wall showered his head with the bright lights and blinking circles of red and green and yellow. The sound was repeated on the far side of the den. Again he dove. Again there was the same rending smash into the sloping, gritty walls. He was bleeding now, and dazed. But he was not beaten. He was not the quitting kind. Not Mudcat Clevenger. "Say something, you damn yellowbelly!" he snarled. "Why don't you say something? I talk. I'm not scairt to talk. You hear me, don't you? Why don't you answer up? It's you, ain't it, Schlonager? You big damn dirty stinking kraut! Make a sound. Let me hear you. I'll cut your yellow-dog heart out! You liar! You sneak! You filthy traitor!"

There was still nothing.

And it grew.

"All right!" The shouting was cracked and wild now. "You think you've got me? You think old Mudcat ain't no more cards to play? Well look at these when I lay 'em down. See how the spots strike you, you lousy squarehead Dutchman! I've got the woman by the throat and I've got the kid's knife and if you don't answer up in a count of five, I'll cut her open like a slaughter shoat!"

The stillness stretched achingly.

"You light the candle again and do it when I count five!" yelled Clevenger, "or I'll slice her. One. Two. Three. Four . . ."

"*Five,*" said the deep voice out of the darkness.

Clevenger whirled toward its source, eyes straining, bugging from his skull-like face. That wasn't Schlonager. That wasn't his soft slow voice. Who was it? Who sounded like that? Scortini? No, he talked high and quick. Was it Squint? Of course not. That cowboy West Texas twang couldn't be hidden even on one word. Harry Albion? The same answer. The Englishman's accent would have coated even the single word with its uppitty tone.

"Pulaski? Bohunkie? Is that you? Answer me, you big dumb slob. It's me, Mudcat. You know old Mudcat, your friend?"

The blackness sounded and resounded. It made noises, fearsome and great, all of its own. But no answer came from it for the straining ears of Mudcat Clevenger.

"Bohunkie, I'll do it, damn you! I'll cut this poor woman's throat. I'll carve her up just like you did your wife, you murdering Polack slob! Answer me, answer me!"

This time there was a soft sound out of the void that surrounded Clevenger; this time an answer came to him.

"That is damn funny," said the thickly spoken tone. "I don't see no woman."

"Pulaski, listen, Bohunkie—" Clevenger broke off

131

his wheedling appeal. Into his coyote's mind had entered another shaft of fear. "What did you say?" he asked the darkness. "What the hell are you talking about, you don't see no woman. You can't see no woman. Not in this hole. You cain't see nothing. Nobody kin."

"I can see *you*," said Pulaski.

Clevenger laughed hoarsely. "Sure, sure," he croaked. "You always was a funny feller, Pulaski. Keep talking . . ."

"You going wrong way," rumbled the Pole.

In his crouching movement toward the sound of his enemy's voice, Clevenger now heard that voice coming from behind him. Damn! The Pole had made a lucky guess. He had moved just as he started for him. "Sure, sure," he said again, "that's right. You got a good brain, Bohunkie. I like you, always did. Pulaski? You hear me?"

"Don't need to hear you," growled the heavy voice. "Why for? I can see you."

Again the sound was off center from where Clevenger had pinned it only the moment before. He lay on the floor of the den, trying to force his mind to lie still and to behave and to think for him.

"What am I doing, Bohunkie?"

"On your belly. Now you look to me. Now you start to me. Now I go."

Clevenger heard the scuttle of the sand grains being moved, then the utter stillness settled again.

"Pulaski? Bohunkie? Now what am I doing?"

"You are still on your belly. Now you got your arm out holding the knife. It lays to your right side, like a snake. You are ready to strike at me."

Clevenger instinctively tensed the arm and hand which lay as the Pole had described it. But he did not withdraw the poised weapon. That Polack slob did not fool him. Of course he could guess that he would be on his stomach. And that he would have the knife ready. And he had to know that he was right-handed. This was just his ghoulish Bohunk sense of being funny. Pulaski had no more brains than an ore-car donkey. That, Clevenger knew. That, he could count on. He tightened his fingers on the haft of the boy's Green River blade. "Pulaski," he said, smiling the words, "I quit. Come on over. I've got the candle here and we can light it up and talk. What you say? Pulaski, you hear me?"

"Sure."

"Well, you coming over?"

"By damn you bet."

There was the scuttle of the sand grains again and then, just when it seemed to the coiled guerrilla knifeman that the movement had nearly reached him, the scuttling stopped.

But now he heard it for the first time.

A man's breathing.

"Pulaski?" He gathered all his muscles, aiming the knife hand. At his call, the breathing shut off. There was nothing, again, as there had been nothing before. Then, as he waited, not breathing himself, there was the last faint rattle of the sand grains. *"Bohunkie? Bohunkie, what are you doing?"* His question went out into the sightless black pleadingly, for the fear, the real fear was in him at last. And the answer came in a way that froze him to his coiled striking pose. And it came from a direction, almost due behind him, which also disrupted his intention and his sense of timing. And with his mind sending cross signals and his ears playing him false and his bulging eyes as sightless as a rockworm's, he lay there the one fatal moment after the Pole's heavy voice replied to him, chillingly, *"I am cutting off the head of the snake. . . ."*

17

WHEN HE HAD CLOSED THE WOLF-DEN ENTRANCE IN THE creek bank, Schlonager ran through the rain toward the stock shed. His heart was pounding from more than the exertion. He did not know if the creek really would rise. He did not know if Clevenger would believe that it would, after he had thought it over. He did not know, above all, what Pulaski was doing at his end of the tunnel. All he was sure of was the simple plan he and the Pole had figured out. And that did not give him much comfort. It had been largely Pulaski's idea to create some fuss at the den mouth while he, Pulaski, crept into the tunnel through the oat bin and came upon a distracted Mudcat Clevenger from the rear. Schlonager knew one other thing, as he ran. It was only a few feet from the oat bin to the part of the tunnel in which the people must be hiding. He was familiar with the denning habit of wolves, and was certain that the denning room would be closer, much closer, to the bank and its entrance, than to the oat bin and its exit. Even so, Pulaski could not have had more than twenty or thirty feet to go, counting turns in the tunnel, and Schlonager had held up Mudcat in conversation for a full four or five minutes during which time it was a certainty that the Pole had not struck at the renegade cavalryman. Skidding in the mud already forming from the sheeting rain, the big sergeant dove in under the shed roof and stood panting beneath the low roof. In a moment, he recovered and dripped his way over the dirt floor to the oat bin. As his hand went to the closed lid and raised it an inch or so, that he might put his ear to the crack and listen for sounds from below, a muffled, wordless cry wrenched its way through the darkness of the tunnel. It was the cry of a wounded beast, and its sobbing, suddenly rising and strangled-off outburst put Schlonager's already straining nerves on the breaking edge. "*My God*," he breathed softly to himself, and crouched there not knowing what to do.

Far down the tunnel, then, he saw the glimmer of light and heard Pulaski's thick voice saying calmly, "That's all right, lady, you come out now. You and kids fine." Followed another sequence of listening seconds during which Schlonager heard nothing. Then it was Pulaski again, telling the woman not to look at something, but to go around it, around the wall of the den,

135

the kids following her and not looking either. The woman replied to him in a low, shaken voice and Schlonager let his wide shoulders sag, knowing, at least, that Mrs. Shuffman and the children were all right and that, somehow, the Pole had done what he went down into that blind hole to do.

He raised the lid all the way and put his boot down into the bin and pushed open the hinged trap bottom of the feed-box and called into the darkness of the tunnel, "Can you hear me, Pulaski? Is everything all right? You want me down there?" He was just making certain and not worried in any way. His instinct was correct. "Sure, you bet. Damn to hell. Be careful, lady. All thing all right now, no hurry . . ." Pulaski's gravel growl, as ugly as his bent and bulbous features, answered at once and with a cheer and good feeling that could not be missed, even strained through thirty feet of wolf tunnel.

In a few moments, young Huff Shuffman appeared out of the hole and waved up to Schlonager with a grin no less wide than the one with which the old sergeant answered it. "Hey, look here!" cried the youngster, turning back over his shoulder to call the good news. "Here's that great big soldier with the gray hair. You know, Maw, the one I told you could whup that Mudcat?" Schlonager heard the woman say something soft and affirmative to the boy, and Huff squeezed out of the tunnel and stood up in the small space Abel Shuffman had hollowed out beneath the oat bin to serve as an entry hall into the narrow lateral of the wolf's runway. "Come on, Maw," he urged, reaching back to take his mother's hand. "There he is; see, right up there at the oat bin." He pointed at Schlonager's looming red face. "Just look at the size of him, will you!"

Behind the boy, Dulcie Shuffman emerged, rubbing the dirt of the tunnel's sides from her eyes. Huff helped her to stand and Schlonager bent down and took her hands and pulled her up into the daylight of the shed. She brushed against him unavoidably in the lifting, and for the first time she and the burly soldier were conscious of her torn blouse. "I'm sorry," she murmured, in a voice that was low and subdued and, somehow, very exciting to Honus Schlonager. "It wasn't easy down there."

He knew that, and he nodded and said, "I reckon, Ma'am," and forced himself to quit staring at her and go back to helping the young girl and the baby and the boy, Huff, up out of the hole. When all were safely lifted to the shed floor, he could hear the nearing grunts of Pulaski making his way out of the tunnel. "What's the matter?" he called sharply to the Pole. "You in some trouble there?"

He heard what he thought was a laugh, then the familiar voice saying all was well but that two could not crawl as simply as one through a hole the size of a stovepipe. There was some more grunting and shuffling and tugging at something, then Pulaski called gruffly, "Send the lady and kids some other place. All right, Sergeant?"

Schlonager replied that it was, and ordered Dulcie Shuffman to take the children and go on up to the main house. "Don't look into the first stall, yonder," he added, remembering suddenly the broken-headed corpse of Ira Shank. "Just head right on past it, Ma'am, and don't be afraid outside. The Sioux are back over the ridge and can't harm you. Everything's going to be fine, now."

The woman nodded in her sober, patient way, thanking Schlonager with her eyes. Reacting, the big sergeant blushed and stood aside, ramrod straight as though on parade, and she and the children filed out of the shed and made their way across the clearing. When he recovered himself from staring after the graceful sway of the widow Shuffman's figure, Pulaski had come out of the tunnel below, and was unbuckling one end of his belt from about his ankle. The other, taut end of the leather stretched into the tunnel behind him. The Pole looked up and bobbed his shaggy head at Schlonager and gave a mighty heave on the belt. Out of the tunnel came the long, booted legs of Mudcat Clevenger. Another grunt, another muscular heave, and the whole body of the guerrilla popped out into the entryway.

Well, almost the whole body.

Around the right forearm, Pulaski had tightly wound a tourniquet made of his neckcloth twisted and tied off hard. Beyond the tourniquet protruded the red pulp of the wrist, and beyond its dirt-clotted stub there was nothing. The right hand was gone.

And yet it wasn't, either.

Pulaski stood up, eyeing Honus Schlonager. He reached inside his shirt and brought out something. "You look for this?" he asked. Schlonager set his teeth. The gritting sound of them was plainly audible. And reasonably so. What Pulaski was holding up toward him was the hairy fist of Mudcat Clevenger, its sinewy dead fingers still spasmed about the handle of Huff Shuffman's Green River knife.

"Yeah," he said, white-lipped, "I guess so. Why in God's name couldn't you have left *that* behind?"

The blond-haired Pole looked up at him, blinking slowly.

"What?" he said. "Leave the boy's knife? Damn to hell. Not right."

"All right," said Schlonager, "bring it along. Leave that other thing down there with the rest of Clevenger."

Pulaski blinked again, shaking his head.

"Can't do that," he mumbled. "Not right to leave Mudcat either."

"What the hell you mean, 'not right'?" said Schlonager quickly. "It'll save us digging another hole, won't it?"

"No," replied the Pole. "Mudcat is not all dead."

"Good Lord!" groaned Schlonager. "Why didn't you finish him while you were about it?"

"I don't know." The question was beyond Pulaski, but it worried him. "Somebody don't let me maybe. Maybe God. Maybe my wife I love. I don't know. You think so?"

"Like as not," said Schlonager uneasily. "Come on, hand him up here. I'm getting jumpy."

"He sure is skinny," said the Pole, feeling the body as he lifted it carelessly. "Like the wet rat chewed by the dog, eh?"

Schlonager had to snort to stop the laugh that wanted, perversely, to come out despite the shiver of revulsion with which he accepted Clevenger's limp form. Hauling the unconscious renegade out of the bin, he let him slip to the dirt floor. When he had helped Pulaski out of the hole and was facing him over the huddled body of Mudcat Clevenger, he nodded and said quietly to the scowling Pole, "One thing you're not, Bohunkie; that's a poet."

Casimir Pulaski neither agreed, nor argued. "Better go, Sergeant," he said. "Boy will want the knife."

"Oh, sure," said Schlonager. "First things first, always." Starting out of the shed, however, he remembered something else. "Hold up," he said to Pulaski, "we got to get rid of Shank." He led the way back to the stall. "Pick him up," he ordered. "We'll dump him down the oat bin. That's as decent as we've time for. Step on it."

Pulaski bent and lifted the body. "Fat," he said.

"Yes," nodded Schlonager. "Fat with hate. You see where it got him."

The Pole bobbed his head. "Fat dead," he growled. "Open up the lid to bin, please. You maybe say some Bible word?"

Schlonager winced at the thumping sound of Ira

140

Shank striking the dirt pit of the wolf hole. He lowered the lid to the oat bin, and nodded grim assent to the request.

"Yeah," he said. "Amen . . ."

18

AS THEY WENT ACROSS THE CLEARING TOWARD THE SOD house the rain began to thin. Nearing the front door of the little cabin, Schlonager paused and looked up toward the south ridge. Pulaski plodded on not noticing his companion had stopped and turned about to study the ridge. Scortini, lounging in the dripping doorway of the cabin, stood aside for the Pole but remained in the door watching the big sergeant.

Schlonager gazed not at the ridge, actually, but at the sky above it. The sun had broken through and arching gracefully over the burnt poles of Crow Mane's burial platform, a gorgeous double rainbow glowed. It seemed to arise at the headwaters of Gooseberry Creek and to reach the earth again just beyond the Big Horn. It was startlingly beautiful and it raised Schlonager's spirits accordingly. "God, that's pretty!" he sighed gratefully, and came about once more toward the house. Scortini continued to watch his approach. He had heard the remark about the rainbow over the ridge but, in the handful of seconds since Schlonager had turned to come toward him, he had noted another distinguishing beauty that had been added to the rocky elevation and that shifted his own practical Sicilian thoughts to a higher level of art appreciation. Still, he felt constrained to acknowledge his sergeant's unexpected awareness of Mother Nature's lovely raiments. The cynical glitter of his dark eyes had the same warm softness of broken glass. "It sure is," he said. "It's purely lovely. I ain't never seen a purtier ridge. Fact is, I ain't seen such lively colors since Crazy Horse tried to take Fort Kearney. Of course, the rainbow's attractive too. Like you said."

Schlonager, who had been letting the ragging enter in one ear and not linger in the other, now stopped dead and said, "What was that?"

"The rainbow," repeated Scortini. "It's pretty *too*."

"That's what I thought you said," nodded Schlonager, and turned back to the ridge. He flinched, but at a greater distance than the doorway the reaction could not have been detected. His round, close-cropped head did not move, but the blue eyes did. They traveled along the crest of the ridge with deliberate slowness, missing no detail of the new chromo now flanking Crow Mane's rain-black funeral pyre. The pigment dimension that had been added to the sun and water color of the rainbow, in the brief moment he had turned away from the ridge, was tremendously effective. Indeed, it was as Scortini had described it—the most compelling array of spotted ponies and war paint since any old Wyoming cavalryman would care to recall. "That's fine," said Schlonager, between his teeth and still studying the ridge. "Just what we needed."

Scortini grinned, his quick monkey's grin. His high voice was laced with mock earnestness. It slid into Schlonager's back like a stiletto. "How many of them did you say there was, Sergeant, sir?" he asked. "I forget."

"I said two dozen," replied the latter evenly. "But that was before the rain."

Scortini eyed his broad back, grinned and shrugged.

"Sure," he said, "that's right. You never can tell what a good rain will bring out from under the rocks, can you?"

"You never can," agreed Schlonager, and turned and came up to the corporal and dropped his voice and asked quietly, "How many do you count this morning, Mario?"

Scortini straightened and squinted at the ridge. His thin lips moved in soundless count. "Maybe sixty," he said. "How about you?"

"Fifty-seven, and I'll guarantee the tally."

"How about the tribe?"

"Mixed. Salts. Straight Oglalas. Hunkpapas. Some Brulé."

"I don't see no Cheyenne nor Arapaho. Do you?"

"No, they're all Cutthroats."

It was the tribal name, their own tribal name, for the Dakota Sioux, taken from their habit of slitting the gullets of their victims as a manner of marking them to the credit of Red Cloud's and Crazy Horse's and Sitting Bull's and Gall's and Hump's, or whoever, bands. Its graphic application did little to amuse Cor-

143

poral Scortini, or to excite his sense of adventure. His fine Sicilian sense of brigandage, however, was touched.

"Do you suppose," he asked Schlonager, "that they would be interested in trading some bright shiny beads, sir?"

"Yes," replied the bear-sized sergeant. "Bright shiny lead ones. Spit out of Spencer carbine barrels. Get inside and start loading, Corporal."

Scortini nodded, taking one last look at the motionless Indian horsemen on the south ridge.

"Whatever you say, Sergeant," he agreed. "But somehow I don't think we're going to make any profit on this swap."

Schlonager paused midway through the low doorway for his own final check of the ridge, before ducking inside.

"You never can tell," he said, going past Scortini.

The Sicilian corporal looked after him. "*Madre!*" he said exasperatedly. "You wouldn't admit water was wet!"

"Not if I was drowning," said Honus Schlonager, and went on into the stifling, tiny room of the sod house.

19

"WHAT TIME IS IT?" ASKED SCHLONAGER. SCORTINI consulted the company watch. "Seven forty," he said. "That makes two minutes and fifteen seconds since we seen the rainbows."

Schlonager glanced up at the half-loft, where he had put Dulcie Shuffman and the children. "You all right up there, Ma'am?" he called. "I know it's close but we can't help it."

"We're fine, Sergeant," the woman answered. "A little close but thankful and not proud."

"Lookit here," said Huff, hanging over the edge to show Schlonager his knife. "I got my Green River back. That there ugly soldier give it to me."

Schlonager winced and looked at Pulaski. The Pole, if he had heard, made no sign. His light eyes were fastened to his rear-wall rifle slit. "That soldier saved your life," he told the boy. "And your Maw's and your two sisters. You'd better remember it."

"Sure," said the boy. "Me and Bohunkie are stout friends. Ain't we, Bohunkie?"

The Pole turned his face toward the loft. "You bet," he said.

Schlonager dropped it. "Mario," he said, "are the Sioux still on the ridge?"

"Just leaving," replied the corporal. "Last ones are starting down right now."

Schlonager wheeled about. "Which side they coming down? Ours?"

"Yes."

"Harry. Squint. Pulaski. Front and center."

He jumped the words at them and the men, surprised, moved away from their rifle slits and came to stand before him.

"Mario, stay on the door. Listen but don't stop

looking. We're going to have to run for the shed. The Sioux are coming down to set up in the timber on the creek and circle the clearing. We've got maybe five minutes to move. Get the horses. Mrs. Shuffman— bring the kids back down. Hurry it."

Harry Albion lounged forward, deliberately loafing.

"I say, Sergeant," he objected, "the shed? Isn't that a bit airy? With that open front and no sods on the roof?"

"We've no choice. Get to those horses."

"But, damn it, Schlonager, it don't make sense!" It was Squint Hibbard, forgetting himself in his excitement over the seemingly absurd order to desert superior cover.

"*Sergeant* Schlonager," said the big N.C.O. flatly.

"All right, all right, damn it, *Sergeant*. But it still don't make sense. Damn the horses. I say we stay here!"

Schlonager hit him on the shoulder, backhanded. It knocked the lanky cowboy sprawling into the cabin wall. He was still blinking and shaking his head when Schlonager took him by the shirt front. "Get a horse," he said quietly.

Squint hesitated, then said sullenly, "Yes, sir," and grabbed the cheek strap of the nearest mount. Schlonager saw that each of the others had a horse similarly in hand, and that each was ready to go. Two horses remained.

"Any Indians yet?" he barked at Scortini.

"No, not clear down, anyway. I see five, six, just

146

past the creek, oh, maybe a quarter mile up it. Others are right back of them. None real close, but coming fast."

Schlonager set his teeth. "All right," he said, "Come on and grab your horse. Mrs. Shuffman, can you run with a horse in one hand? I mean with your skirt to hobble you and, well, you know, being a woman and all."

Dulcie Shuffman gave the baby to Marybell. She pulled her dress up and tucked it in the ties of her apron. Her legs were long and well shaped. The soldiers looked at the white round thighs and did not think of Indians for a moment. Schlonager nodded, embarrassed, but proud of the woman.

She caught his look and responded to it. "Certainly, I can run," she said. "Who will take the baby?"

"Me," said Schlonager, and took the tiny bundle from the older girl. "Huff, you all set to make a dash for the stock shed? It'll be a better Indian fight down there. More room to shoot, and all. Everybody ready? Let's go—"

He led the way, Huff galloping at his side, Dulcie and Marybell Shuffman running behind him and ahead of the soldiers with the other four horses. It seemed to Schlonager as though the distance across the clearing had grown to a mile, but they made the shed with thirty seconds to spare. A handful of the Sioux saw the last of them dash into it, and came on the flat gallop to cut them off but were of course too late and only fired their Winchesters to show their good intentions and not with any serious thought of damage.

"Keep them off of the house!" shouted Schlonager, handing the baby to Dulcie Shuffman. "Make them think we've got something in there worth defending. It'll take their minds off us down here for a spell."

The men fired, driving the Indians back out of the clearing and away from the sod-roofed cabin. They went with no more than a few shouts and war whoops of derision and a scattering of shots thrown high over the shed and for effect only, after the Indian fashion of retreating from any field. "Hold fire!" yelled Schlonager, lowering his own Spencer. "They won't be back for a couple of hours."

The men, taking small relief from this prediction, came up to stand around him and to wait for him to explain what in the name of sweet reason they were doing here in the stock shed instead of being safely up at the thick-walled main house. Schlonager understood what they were thinking and why they stood as they did, accusing him with every look and pose of their company. He cleared his throat and spat into the dirt of the floor.

"We'll start," he said, "with one simple fact of life."

He waited a few moments, letting the silence grow and the carbine smoke curl up under the low pole ceiling and allowing the men time to get uncomfortable.

"Now, then," he suggested, "look at it this way.

Here we have water for man and beast, which we can get through the wolf-hole tunnel, and which the Sioux don't know a thing about. It's turning off hot again today as you can surely feel already. If it goes two, three hot days in a row and all of us with no water—especially the kids—you can get the idea of what would start happening. All the Indians need do is sit and smoke their kinnikinnick and lie their lies and gamble the sticks and let us dry out. They get—all of us—without another shot. Now, I could make a lot longer speech and go into all sorts of side reasons for preferring to shoot from this shed, wet, than from that cabin, dusty. But I won't. If a man of you can think of a better reason than water for making that run just now, you name it for me and I'll go along with you. I'm sorry I didn't have time to put it to a vote, boys, but if we had waited three minutes up there we would still be there. And we would still be there tomorrow morning at this time. And the next morning after that. And the next and the next and the next. The only difference between us and those others up there would be that they're under the floor and we would be on top of it. If I've failed to make my position clear, please feel free to raise the question. Fact is, I'll raise it for you: *who don't like to drink?*"

The men looked at one another. He had stretched the speech deliberately long, so that they would have time to think about it. He knew he was right, but bone-weary and hopeless and very frightened men are seldom able to stop and think straight. He had stopped these and he was hoping they would have been held long enough to see reason.

They had been.

"Why, hell," drawled Squint Hibbard, "where'd you ever get any idea we was agin you, Sergeant? I personally am a very heavy drinker from a'way back. Love the stuff."

"Cheers, cheers," said Harry Albion. "I use it myself when I can't come upon whiskey. It's splendid for tidying up dishes, as well, and absolutely essential, I understand, for potted geraniums."

Scortini shrugged. "Yeah," he said, "me too."

Pulaski not denying that he also needed water to survive, Schlonager nodded and went on. "All right," he said, "let's police-up this shed and then hold a staff meeting."

"How about the Sioux?" asked Squint.

"They'll be doing the same thing," Schlonager told him. "Council of war going on right this minute, I will bet you. But they won't vote to do anything desperate in the middle of the day. Dawn and dusk you can look for them. Otherwise, no trouble. Smart, you see, like animals. They lay up while the sun's overhead and hammering hard."

"You know something, Honus," said Scortini, "you're developing into quite a speaker. I ain't heard you talk so much since that time we took on them Texas trail hands down in Abilene. Ah, me! those were the days. You remember that redheaded Mexican girl with the—"

"Shut up!" cried Schlonager. "I don't know what you're talking about. Whoever heard of a redheaded Mexican?"

"That's what I said when you told me about her," began Scortini, "but, by God, she was sure enough red—"

This time Schlonager said, "*Corporal* Scortini, shut up!" and rolled his desperate blue eyes toward the interested Dulcie Shuffman and her children, promising in the glance a longer, harsher death for Mario Scortini than any the Sioux might furnish him, unless he forthwith ceased and desisted and, moreover, put some of the dirt back into the hole he had just dug under Sergeant Honus Schlonager.

"Sure, sure!" laughed the Sicilian. "What's the matter with everybody? Can't a fellow have a little fun around here? You birds afraid of Indians, or something? I was just funning about that redhaired Mexican girl. Hell, anybody knows Mexicans don't have red hair. Matter of fact, this girl had black hair. It hung clear to her—"

Schlonager grounded his carbine butt on the dirt floor of the shed with wicked force. The effect was dramatic, too, for between the steel-shod butt and the hard earth reposed the right toe of Corporal Mario Scortini's boot. The cry that flew outward from the stock shed was piercing and the Sicilian war dance, as staged by the cursing corporal with but one leg to hop about on, was the rival of anything Siouxian or Cheyenne or Arapahoan.

"Pulaski," said Schlonager, "I want you to go down in the hole and get rid of Shank. Take the shovel and clear out the bank hole and shove him into the creek. The water is up and moving fast from the storm. It will take him away quick and far."

The Pole nodded, took the shovel, headed for the oat bin. Huff Shuffman jumped after him. "I'll go along with you, Bohunkie!" he cried. "You mighten need a helper with a good knife down there."

Schlonager reached out and caught the boy by the shirt-tail. He hauled him back abruptly.

"You'll do the duty you're assigned to, Huff," he told him sternly. "We don't play any favorites in the United States Cavalry. You hear me?"

Huff looked at him uncertainly a moment. Then he nodded, impressed, and said quickly, "Yes, sir!" and saluted and stood at what he imagined was attention.

"At ease, soldier," waved Schlonager, and turned to Dulcie Shuffman. "Ma'am," he asked, "did you ever do much nursing, uh, handle anybody that was bad hurt?"

The sod-house woman smiled her patient smile.

"You don't live in this land with a family of three kids and not learn about nursing and accidents and such. You're going to clean up that soldier—Clevenger—is that it, Sergeant? I saw that his hand was gone. You'll have to cauterize the stump, of course. He'll be bad for a spell, but he's terrible strong. He'll gain back fast. I've seen worse than that sitting up and arguing inside half an hour."

"Yes," said Schlonager, "I know."

"We'll need boilt water," said the woman. "There's a bucket in the wagon stall. Somebody will have to set a fire going. We must find a piece of iron to heat cherry-red for the sealing, too. Then, we'll need . . ."

She hesitated, conscious of the fact that the huge gray-haired sergeant was grinning at her, and that his vivid blue eyes in the tanned, weather-cracked face were looking at her with some feeling more intense than the amusement that was crinkling the attractive crow's-feet on his homely smile. She blushed deeply, and Honus Schlonager saluted her and said, "Yes, Ma'am, Captain Shuffman, Ma'am, we will get to it right away," and both of them laughed and felt wonderfully the better for everything they had exchanged in that moment that had come a little late in life for each of them.

20

THEY HEATED THE IRON-CAPPED END OF THE BROKEN whiffletree to the proper color and sealed off the stump of Clevenger's wrist without the use of water. Schlonager had decided it was too risky lowering the bucket to the stream from the bank hole in daylight. They would have to wait for water until dark. If suffering from thirst became severe enough before then, they would chance the action, but they would not do it for Mudcat Clevenger's comfort or safety. The latter made no complaint. He knew enough of battle wounds to know that if the stump were not sterilized and its arteries closed cleanly, he would develop infection, probably gangrene, and be dead in swift hours. "Get on with it," he had gritted to Schlonager. "I ain't afeared."

Now he lay in the wagon stall beyond the small fire of the surgery, Schlonager crouched above him with the still hissing whiffietree in his hand. The sergeant threw the cauterizer from him and said to the hovering Dulcie Shuffman, "All right, wrap it up good and tight on the stub end, but not back up the wrist too far. Make him a sling for it, if you've got the cloth to do so."

The woman nodded. She removed her petticoat, while the silent soldiers watched, and tore it into strips for the bandaging. "There's cloth enough," she answered Schlonager. "You did real good with that iron, Sergeant. Saved his life, likely—" She began tying off the wrist, and Schlonager returned the nod awkwardly.

"You do pretty good with that bandage, too, Ma'am," he said. "Real good. Maybe we ought, you and me, to go into the business." She gave him a brief glance, went on with the wrapping. Clevenger, conscious all the while, groaned in pain, and she pushed him back and said a soft word to comfort him. He was grateful for it, clearly. Schlonager wondered at his fierce vitality. He tried to say something else to Dulcie Shuffman, but couldn't. He backed away and walked over to Scortini, on post at the open front of the shed.

"Anything?" he asked.

Scortini shrugged. "Well, yes," he said, "that blue smoke looks real pretty rising above those dark green pines and backed by the yellow of the river bluff. I guess you'd say that was something. Why in the hell do they always build a fire? They can't light down to tighten a cinch buckle but what they have to scrape up a pile of sticks and set it going."

"Fire," said Schlonager, "is something that goes with men, that's all. It's instinct, I guess. It gives confidence. You know, Mario, there's more to warm about a man than his hands."

"Like what?"

"His inside self."

"Schlonager, Honus A.; Doctor of Philosophy and Applied Soothing Syrup," said Scortini acridly. "Now we've got the noble red man gifted with a soul, just like he was human. What will you think of next, O great white friend of the timid wild brother?"

"You asked me why they built fires all the time. I'm telling you. It's to warm their hearts and minds. It helps them think. It leads them to talk. And that's two things they do in reverse order to the white man. They think first. We blat out anything that comes to tongue."

"In simple English that any hard-working Sicilian boy can understand, then, they're squatting over there deciding which way to slit our windpipes, right to left, or left to right, eh?"

"That's about as simple as you can make it."

"I wasn't being so smart, then, saying the smoke over the trees was worth reporting."

"No, not too smart."

"Well, what next?"

"We had better build some fire of our own."

"And do some thinking, eh?"

"Right. As soon as Pulaski gets out of the hole, put Mrs. Shuffman and the kids back down in it, and we'll have us a powwow of our own."

Scortini frowned. "You mean it; putting them back down there? How come?"

Schlonager looked out over the clearing, toward the Sioux smoke rising above the bull pines. "Mario," he said, "you know how much good it's going to do for us to hold a talk, don't you? You've been seven years in Wyoming with me. You know those people over there well enough to realize the general trend of their thinking. If you were them and you had four Pony Soldiers and a cripple and a comely white woman and a young virgin girl and a fine boy of only eight summers—just right to make a good Sioux of—what would you be saying to your brothers over there just now? Would you be advising a gentle retreat? Bearing in mind that it's fifty miles to Fort Pitchfork, seventy-five to Fort McKinney, and not much more to where Sitting Bull wiped out Custer last year? And bearing in mind that if they take us, they take not only the women and the fine young boy, but ten brand-new Spencer repeating carbines, plus mine and yours and Lieutenant Gilliam's Colt revolvers, and ammunition in plenty for all of same?"

Scortini thought of it a long moment.

"Like I said earlier," he grinned, "you are turning into a first-rate talker. I think you could get elected on the Abraham Lincoln ticket in Tuscaloosa, Alabama."

"If those Sioux decide to come for us," went on the other, "there isn't anything in the world we can do but hold them off for the first couple of rushes. After that, they will take this shed and everything in it."

"Only," said Scortini, "the woman and her kids won't be in it. They'll be down that wolf hole. Right?"

"Right. Can you improve on the idea?"

"No. But what's to keep the Indians from discovering the oat-bin entrance, the same as you and me did?"

"Nothing except straight luck. I figure if they take us and the shed, that the division of our guns and horses will get their minds off wondering about the Shuffmans. Besides, there's the good chance they didn't see the family with us. We might have gotten them from the main house, down here, without any of the Sioux saw them."

"I doubt that, but there's a chance, like you say."

"Yes, it's better than if they were in the shed with us. They may get clean away. Its not too far a march down the Big Horn to Greybull. They can make it easy after the Sioux have decided us and gone on home."

"You make it sound slick as a Kansas City snake oil salesman," said the corporal. "Do you want flowers at your funeral, or the money donated to some worthy cause?"

157

"I didn't say we *couldn't* make it," muttered Schlonager. "I just said you'd never get rich and retire taking bets on it. Let's go, there's Pulaski coming out of the bin. You get Squint and Harry. I'll handle the others."

The optimism was premature.

The "others" did not wish to be handled.

"Sergeant," said Dulcie Shuffman, when he had told her what he wanted, "I can shoot a gun from the shoulder as well as most men. I saw those Indians. There are more than plenty of them. Now, I want to stay up here with you."

She had moved forward and spoken low voiced, so that the children would not hear. Schlonager replied in kind.

"You saw the Indians, Ma'am," he said, "but we're not certain they saw you. Long as there's the chance they didn't, we've got to keep you and the kids out of sight."

"The children, yes. Marybell's old enough. She can lead the way to Greybull, if all goes well. But not me. I want to fight."

"You can't do it," said Schlonager, hard-faced. "Look at our side of it. If they see a woman, they'll only come at us the more wicked. You've lived in this country, Ma'am. You know I'm leveling with you."

The woman dropped her head. "I still want to stay up here and help," she murmured. "You will need all the guns you can get. And you know I'm leveling with you, Sergeant Schlonager."

"Yes, Ma'am, that's so. We are short. But there's no sense waving a red rag in front of these Sioux bulls. You'll have to go below with the kids. Besides, Ma'am, there's the baby. Huff said she was sickly. Now, she will surely need you."

"No," said Dulcie Shuffman, "Marybell can take care of her, or she can stay up here with me. We can put her on the hay pile. She sleeps mostly anyways."

"I heard her cry." Schlonager shook his head. "If I can hear her, so can the Sioux. She'll have to go down the hole, and you with her, Ma'am." He reached to take her arm, but was interrupted by Scortini's voice calling him over to the oat bin. He went over and found the corporal scowling angrily at Casimir Pulaski. The latter was shaking his head as though to deny guilt of any degree, and Schlonager said wearily, "All right, now what?" and Scortini palmed his hands in Latin helplessness and answered, "My God, don't ask me, ask that idiot!"

Schlonager looked at the Pole.

"Nothing," said Pulaski. "I don't do nothing."

"Exactly!" yelled Scortini. "You send him down that hole to get rid of Shank so that we can send Mrs. Shuffman and the kids down there to hide, and what happens? Nothing! All he does is dig out the hole to the bank then stick his stupid head up here and grunt, 'Wot wuz it the Sergeant say to do with Shank?' Honest to God, Honus, I'm going to kill me a Bohunkie, before some dirty Sioux does me out of the pleasure!"

"Simmer down," said Schlonager, "there's no harm done."

"Sure," said Pulaski, helpfully. "Shank, he don't care."

"All right," said Scortini, "that does it. A Polish comedian. I was wondering what it was that we needed to round out our little troop, and now I know. A murdering dumb slob of a Polack humorist. I will bet you that you were a sensation in South Pittsburgh, eh Bohunkie? What act did you follow? The trick dogs or the trained bears?"

"That's enough," said Schlonager. "Shank doesn't make any difference one way or the other."

Behind them, they were conscious of the rustle of skirting and that indefinable but absolute "feel" of the presence of the female with a company of rough men.

"Maybe Shank does make a difference, Sergeant," said Dulcie Shuffman in her low, husky voice. "How big was he—the dead soldier down there, I mean?" she added, pointing to the oat bin and the tunnel opening.

"How big was Shank?" repeated Schlonager. "What do you mean, Ma'am?"

"I mean could I wear his uniform and look right in it?"

Scortini and Pulaski stared at the woman, as though the heat or the strain had gotten her, but Honus Schlonager felt the tingle of admiration for her quick wit and steady courage spread through him like a downing of straight bourbon. "Ma'am," he said quietly, "I think you'd look about right in Shank's uniform. How about your hair?"

Dulcie Shuffman shrugged. "There's horse shears in the harness box," she said, pointing to a wall bracket above the oat bin. "You can cut it off, while they're getting the clothes for me. And, Sergeant—" she fixed him with her luminous gray eyes, "I want to thank you."

"Do you mean," said Scortini, breaking in incredulously, "that she's going to soldier alongside of us?"

"*She* means it," said Schlonager.

"Oh, my God!" said the little Sicilian. "Now we've got female Indian fighters!"

Honus Schlonager said nothing, but Dulcie Shuffman's compelling voice caught at Scortini and held him fast.

"Out here," she said, "in this lonely, Godforsaken land, you've always had female Indian fighters, Corporal. Without them, there'd be no Fort Pitchfork, no Pony Soldiers, no Sergeant Schlonagers. You take away the women that have shouldered arms in Wyoming, and you'd be all alone out here with General Custer and the buffaloes . . ."

Scortini stared at her.

He gave her a good, long, hard look.

Then he grinned and saluted.

"Yes, sir, Ma'am," he said. "Come on, Bohunkie, back in the hole. We got us a new recruit to outfit!"

THE MEETING OF SCHLONAGER WITH HIS CORPORAL AND three troopers was brief. It was held when Scortini and Pulaski had returned with Shank's uniform, and while Dulcie Shuffman was still below ground getting her children resettled in the wolf's den. The five men sat on their haunches in the open front of the shed. As they talked they scanned the bull pines where the Sioux smoke still curled, or let their restless glances stray to the creek timber. Nothing was to be seen of the Indians in either reach of cover. True to Schlonager's prediction, they were in no hurry. Or so it seemed.

"Harry," said the big German sergeant, "let's start with you. How high did you get in the British Army?"

"Eh?" said the Englishman, startled.

"You've been an officer." It was a flat statement, admitting of no evasive maneuver. Harry Albion moved his hands futilely. "I've been many things, Sergeant. Among them a lieutenant in Her Majesty's service." He paused, grimacing. "I wasn't out there long. India, you know. Not cut out for the job, really. Funked and ran the first time under fire. Up in the Khyber country, it was. They sent me home, disgraced, naturally. I came over here. Quite a short story, I think. Why do you ask?"

"I thought you might have something to say about this situation. Tactics are not my dish. If you've been to school, maybe they taught you something we could apply here. I think you could call this a tactical situation, couldn't you? It certainly isn't the sort of surround where ordinary measures will work. Were you in cavalry?"

"No, I think it was Karachi," smiled the Englishman. Then, seeing his light touch was not appreciated, he waved his slender hands again. "Yes, Bengal Lancers," he said. "But that's no good here. Not really."

"Cavalry's cavalry," said Schlonager. "Have you got any ideas to get us out of this jam, foot or horse?"

"No."

Schlonager turned from him to Scortini. "Mario?" he said.

The corporal frowned, lowered his head. "Nothing," he mumbled, ashamed.

"Squint?"

The cowboy scraped his bristled chin with his left hand, studied the pines again. "Naw," he decided. He was not unhappy about it, like Scortini. Not about the decision itself. About being trapped by half a hundred horse Indians, he was hardly pleased. But insofar as any moral issues over his failure to have an answer for his sergeant, Squint Hibbard was unmoved. He would shoot when the time came to shoot. Killing Indians or getting killed by them was the same as sticking up stagecoaches for a living. A man took his chances.

"Pulaski?" said Schlonager.

The Pole shrugged. His brutal face with its low-

163

growing coarse blond hair and staring pale eyes held the expression of a Neanderthal hunter crouched in a cave's mouth twenty centuries removed. He had no words at all, and only shook his head and kept on staring.

Now Schlonager did a thing that surprised them all.

Without turning, he threw his voice over his shoulder, toward the wagon stall directly behind them. "Clevenger," he called, "you listening to this? What do you say? You got any guerrilla ideas to get us out of here? What would Bloody Bill have done? Or Quantrill? Or Barney Poole?"

All the men were watching Mudcat now, except Schlonager, who continued to keep his back to him. The renegade raised himself to the elbow of his left arm. His eyes glared savagely from the sockets which pain and shock had sunk ever deeper into the narrow skull. He seemed to be gathering himself to rage at the sergeant in some obscene anger of hatred. But, suddenly, a gleam of craft and caution diverted the fury, and his answer left them all wondering.

"Lemme think," said Clevenger. "God, but I am sick, boys, and this arm hurts fiercely bad, but I want to do something, iffen I am able, to make it up to you all, and also to them poor little kids and their brave Maw. Leave me have just a little time, Schlonager; I'll try to think for you."

"Sure," said the big sergeant, and sat silently frowning.

The others watched him a few moments, then Scortini said, "Well, Honus, how about you? We're all anxious to hear from the expert."

The men muttered eagerly in agreement, and waited for him to answer the corporal. No matter what had passed before, from doubt to suspicion to open rebellion, they were, in this final accounting, back to where they had been at the outset of the mission—back to believing in Sergeant Honus Schlonager. The latter did not miss this swift return to an original trust, nor was he confused by it. *All that a man has will he give for his life.* These men had nothing. And that was exactly what they were giving Schlonager.

"All right," he said softly, "I'll tell you how it looks to me, and what I think we must do."

Quickly, quietly, he made clear that the immediate problem was to survive until nightfall. He was certain the Sioux would make an attack at dusk, or sunset, and that they would do it in their familiar style of the mounted rush, not by circling as they did with trapped wagons or isolated buffalo hunters on the open prairie. The shed was not of thin canvas and fragile wagon spokes. It was solid log and pole construction. Circling it and shooting at it from the offside of a galloping mustang would prove a total waste of powder and lead, as well as of pony flesh. Schlonager thought the Indians would not be in this mood. If he knew exactly what Sioux those were that had joined the Salts, he could make a better guess as to how hard the rush would be pushed. But he had a feeling those were bad Indians, or they wouldn't be down in this part of the country at this particular time. With the army on the hunt for the Custer killers who might drift down out of Canada, and still in pursuit of Crazy Horse and his hostile Oglala who had remained at large in the United States, it wasn't likely that the new joiners over there in the bull pines would be peacefully inclined. It was only wise of Schlonager and his soldiers to act according to his, Schlonager's, educated guess, the sergeant concluded, and that would be for them to be ready for the sunset or early dusk rush of the shed by combined Sioux force. Beating off that rush, when it came, and so winning through to darkness still in possession of the shed, provided them with the sole true chance they had—any of them—to live.

The troopers sat frowning after he had finished the preliminary statement. It was Harry Albion who furnished the obvious yeast to leaven the rest of the loaf.

"I say," he queried plaintively, "didn't you leave something out, Sergeant? I mean, it was a lovely review up to a point, but you forgot the bloody point, eh what?"

"The point?" said Schlonager.

"Yes, you know, the answer; the blooming Rosetta stone."

"The blooming what?" asked Schlonager.

"Rosetta stone, old chap: a piece of black basalt found in 1799 near the Rosetta mouth of the Nile, bearing a bilingual inscription in hieroglyphics, demotic characters and Greek, famous as having given the Frenchman M. Champollion the first clue toward deciphering the Egyptian writings. Really quite some important rock, you know."

"Harry," said Schlonager, eyeing him, "I went to the fourth grade in Wisconsin. Not through it, just to it. We didn't get to the Rosetta stone. We didn't even get to the Nile. All I remember about Egypt is a picture of Cleopatra aerating her belly button on a cigar band. Now, if you'd care to come again with your complaint about me and my poor memory for points, I'll give it a whirl on that basis."

Private Harry Albion winced and saluted the burly German. "Well spoken, O mighty Caesar," he said. "The Moving Finger writes, and having writ, moves on. I see its cabalistic cipher engraven on the Rock of Time. I see the Rosy Key appear and unlock the secret meanings of the message. Its words stand forth in letters of fire and brimstone. They are simple words. Simple even to the exalted level of an American sergeant of mounted troops of the frontier. They say: 'Having led his heroes to the saving shade of Ebon Night, and beaten off successfully the savage Foe, what then proposes Mighty Schlonager'?"

"How's that, Harry?" demanded the questioned one.

"*What the hell do we do when it gets dark?*" answered the Englishman laconically.

Schlonager bit down on it hard. He chewed doggedly but it would not masticate. Finally, he spat it out dejectedly.

"That's a good question," he admitted.

There was another of those stretching pauses

becoming so familiar to them all in the past hours; then Harry Albion said, in his brittle way, "Well, I've got a good answer for it, should you care to hear it."

"Go on," said Schlonager.

"I know it works," nodded Albion, "for I have previously tried it myself."

"Go on," repeated Schlonager, tensing.

"Cut and run," shrugged the Englishman. "Grab a bloody horse and get out. Go when it's dark and go like hell."

Schlonager didn't answer him, but looked to the others.

Scortini met his gaze by turning his own to the five cavalry horses tied hard and fast in Shuffman's stalls.

"There's one apiece," he said.

Squint Hibbard said, "I get the same count."

Pulaski said nothing.

"What about Mrs. Shuffman and the kids?" asked Schlonager with hard-eyed slowness. "What about the little boy? The older girl? That sick baby? What about them?"

"You said it yourself, Sergeant," answered Private Harry Albion. "They have a better chance in the blooming hole than we do in the bloody shed. Your own words, not mine."

His wide English eyes were as hard as Schlonager's, and Hibbard and Scortini backed him with their narrowed glances. Only Pulaski sat uncommitted, hands knotted between his knees, blond head hung down and staring at the dirt floor. Schlonager still spoke very slowly.

168

"That's only providing the Sioux don't know that they retreated to this shed with us. If they saw them, then—" He didn't finish it, and didn't need to finish it.

It was Squint Hibbard who got up first.

The cowboy looked at the Sioux campfire smoke across the clearing, then back to the crowded cavalry horses in the shed beyond him.

"I still count five horses," he said, and picked up his Spencer carbine and went back to his rifle slit.

22

WHEN THE SUN WAS STRAIGHT OVERHEAD, THREE Indians rode out of the bull pines and halted their ponies.

Scortini, dozing on guard in front of the shed, called the one word *"company!"* to Honus Schlonager, and the big sergeant roused himself from where he rested against the wagon stall partition, and came forward. When the Sioux saw him they called over in their deep voices, *"Shone-ih-gah!"* and held their rifles over their heads in both hands.

"That's as close as they can come to my name," said Schlonager. "They're like Chinamen; they have trouble with l's and r's." He moved away from Scortini, into the grass of the clearing, and held up his carbine in the same manner. "What do you want?" he asked them in Sioux.

"To talk," said the middle one. "We'll put the guns on the ground."

"All right. I will do the same."

Schlonager laid his Spencer on the grass. The three Sioux got down off their ponies and put their Winchesters carefully on three stumps which Shuffman had logged off. They came slowly toward the big white man. He began moving to meet them. They came together precisely midway of the saucer of meadow grass.

"I am Taopi Kte, Little Killer," said the wizened, small brave who was the leader. "These are Falling Leaf on my left, and Quick Horse on my right. We speak for the Miniskuya, the Salt Band, Crow Mane's people."

"You know me," said Schlonager.

"Yes, Shone-ih-gah, friend of Crow Mane. I remember you from the time you stayed with us, when you were hurt. Do you remember me?"

"Yes," said Schlonager, uneasily. "I believe you are the boy's uncle. The brother of his mother."

"True, he was my nephew. The only one."

"He was like a son to you, then?"

"Yes, you know that."

"And you know that I'm sorry he was killed. That soldier who killed him is a bad man. I have him under arrest and will put him on trial for murdering your nephew."

"Many are put on trial," said the wrinkled Sioux. "Few are taken away to the jail. Is this not so?"

"It is so," admitted Schlonager. "What do you want?"

"We only want to say, like brave men, that we honor the way you buried Crow Mane. You were his friend, it is true. So we will do the same for you."

"You'll burn me, eh?"

"Yes."

"Meanwhile, while you are doing this honorable thing of telling me about it, you are also getting a good look into my shed over there and counting my men and seeing how good their hearts look and how ready they are with their guns, eh? Very smart. You don't fool Schlonager."

The tall Indian pushed forward one step. He struck himself on the chest, left-handedly. "We don't have to fool you. We have the power. We have the big *hmunha,* the real magic to hurt you. Sixty men. All warriors of reputation."

"Fifty-seven men," corrected Schlonager. "And at least one of them a long, skinny-boned, loud talker."

The Indian flushed and drew back his feathered eagle-bone whistle, as though he would strike the white sergeant with it. Then, he controlled himself. "It's true," he said, "I talk a lot. Tonight, I'll be talking to your scalp drying over our fires, there, beyond the pine trees."

"Tonight," said Schlonager quietly, "is many hours from this time. I, too, know something that will happen tonight. Absolutely and without fail. You will see."

The fat brave now stepped up to him. He was the sly one, the thinker, the one with the devious mind.

"Eh? What is that?" he smiled, showing that he was a good fellow and wouldn't hurt a fly. "What is it that you know will happen absolutely and without fail tonight?"

"It will get dark," said Schlonager.

The fat Sioux turned a little pale. He stood to his full height, a little over his total circumference. "My name is Tashunka Luza," he said. "I will remember your sharp tongue. I will cut it out of your head for you."

"They should call you Slow Mare, not Quick Horse," said Schlonager, poking a forefinger into the roll of suet that encircled the Indian's gee-string top. "You are big enough to drop twin foals and so poor in your thinking that I am ashamed to let your friends see us talking together. Kindly look the other way, will you, and behave as though we were standing in two different meadows?"

The other two Sioux burst out laughing and began probing Quick Horse's pendulous abdomen with their own fingers and making suggestive remarks about his manhood and when he was expecting the little one and if he had a name picked for it yet, and so on. Then, as quickly, the laughter was shut off and the little brave was back to Honus Schlonager. "It's nice you have a sense of humor," he told him. "We Sioux appreciate that. A good laugh aids the digestion. When the calf dies happy the meat is sweet. Keep telling the jokes. *Hookahey!*"

"Wait a moment," called Schlonager, holding up his

right hand. "Would you care to tell a brother which Indians those are who have ridden in to join you? You know how it is in a good fight. You like to know who is your enemy. Some are proud, others are not."

"These are pretty proud," answered Little Killer readily. "They are all from the camp of Crazy Horse. Crazy Horse has gone in and surrendered to the soldiers. They say he will go to Fort Robinson. They say they will not hurt him but these Indians don't believe that. They think Crazy Horse will be killed. They are fleeing to Canada, but hunting on the way. They are bad Indians."

Schlonager nodded grimly. "You scarcely needed to add that," he said. "If they are running from the soldiers, they are very bad Indians. Why don't you leave them while there is time? Go on home with your Salts. If we live to get out of here, we will stand up for you, we will say you did what you could to help us. In view of the soldiers of mine whom you killed at the Cottonwood Rocks, this could be a very good idea. You know Captain Hobart at my fort. You know how he will act when he hears what you have already done. You will need white friends."

"That's true," admitted Little Killer. "But we don't plan to stay down here either. We will go to Canada with those others over there. They want to go with us. We have already told them it is all right. Besides, we have taken the vow to do for you what you have done for Crow Mane. Would you have us go back on our words?"

"No," said Schlonager, "never that."

He knew that it was over. They had come, those three simple-minded sons of the high plains, just as they said, to warn him as brave warriors that they intended to take his hair and stretch his corpse on a burning platform. To linger longer in talk would be useless, and might be dangerous. It was a favorite trick of theirs to violate a truce meeting. They had learned this art from experts. They had learned it from the white men. So it was time to go. Except for one thing.

"My brother," said Schlonager to Little Killer, "when he was dying, Crow Mane gave me his word that you had not seen the white woman and her children. As I was sent out here by my captain to find this woman and those children, you will understand my feelings for them. I would die easier in my mind, could I know their fate. If it were you in my place—did you look for a brother's squaw and her young ones—I would tell you what I knew of them, or if I knew nothing of them I would also tell you this. How say you?"

Little Killer shrugged quickly.

"I say you are right. I will tell you all I know of those people. Nothing. We didn't even see them. They must have gotten out by a boat, down the river. An Indian from the reservation told us Shuffman had a boat hidden here somewhere. We couldn't find it. So it is gone and no doubt that woman took her children in it and got out."

"*Ho-ha,*" said Schlonager gravely, "thank you. I think Crow Mane's spirit will rest more easily too for that kindness of yours. I salute you. The Salts are proud."

Little Killer touched the fingers of his left hand to his forehead. It was the respect salute of the Sioux. "*Woyuoni-han,*" he answered Schlonager, "I return the word. You are proud too. Fight good, Shone-ih-gah."

Schlonager touched his brow in turn.

"The same to you, Taopi Kte," he said. "May all your mares drop buffalo horses."

The three Sioux turned and started for their ponies. Of a sudden, Little Killer stopped and came back. He peered up at Schlonager a moment, then said "*hau,*" and put out his hand and added in halting English, and with vehement sincerity, "Hey! Hell with everything. We shake hands . . ."

Schlonager took the small red hand in both his huge hands and pressed it warmly and without awkwardness. No more words were exchanged. Nor was anything altered by the curious action. The next time that Schlonager saw Little Killer it was over the sights of a Spencer carbine.

23

THE HEAT IN THE SHED WAS AS SMOTHERING AS THAT IN the sod-house cabin. Some air moved in the structure, but it was hot. The day, outside, was building to be worse than the one before. The rain had intensified the humidity. It was like a blanket wrung out in boiling water and swathed about the head and face. Breathing seemed a real emergency. By three o'clock the horses, which had not been properly watered for twenty-four hours, were drooping in the stalls. They were going down rapidly and to delay further the risk of going through the tunnel to the creek would be to add the risk of not having useable mounts if and when the moment of escape might arise.

At four o'clock, when Scortini awakened Schlonager from an hour's cat nap, the temperature was higher than ever. Men and mounts ran sweat in rivers. The crusted salt of this perspiration stood in small bluffs and channel edgings on the hides of the horses. The men licked desperately at the saline drops that ran from their own faces, then cursed and spat and rubbed cottony, swollen lips. Schlonager knew the time was then.

"Mario," he said, "get me the bucket."

"Let me go," said Scortini. "I'm smaller and can get through that hole easier and faster."

"No. We can't take a chance on them rushing the place while the two of us are underground. You stay up here."

"All right. Say hello to Dulcie for me."

Schlonager glanced at him quickly, but he was grinning his old brigand's grin and the big sergeant could not be angry with him. Particularly where he had a legal right to the grin, if an immoral one.

"You may have forgotten it," he told him, "but my orders concerned that woman and those kids. I haven't been down the hole yet and I consider it my duty to give it the once over. That's in case we have to use it getting out of here tonight."

"You still think you're fooling anybody about getting out of here tonight? Or any other night?"

"No, I'm not fooling anybody. I mean it."

"Go on down the hole. Maybe you can sell that line of gospel talk to the lady. It ain't my style."

"Get me the bucket," repeated Schlonager. "And watch out sharp while I'm gone."

Scortini brought him the bucket. "I want you to take a look at how Shuffman figured out to put the oats and corn in the bottom of that bin after it is closed," he said. "Look at this—"

He slipped down into the bin ahead of Schlonager and called up, "Now, watch."

He let the bin bottom spring up in place. Then Schlonager saw one of the pieces of milled lumber in the back of the bin slide to one side. Out came Scortini's hand full of oats and corn and sprinkled them upon the bottom of the bin and withdrew to slide the fitted board back into perfect place. The bin bottom then opened again and the corporal climbed up into the shed. "How do you like that?" he said. "You can use the sliding board from up here to also set and unset the latch that holds the bin bottom firm if you press on it or step on it from up here. No wonder the damn Sioux never outsmarted this Shuffman!"

Schlonager said, "They outsmarted him once."

"Where was that?" asked Scortini, not thinking.

"Over on the Tensleep Trail," said Schlonager, and the corporal said, "Go to hell and take your hand bucket with you. I'll leave the lid open so you can see to find the tunnel. Good luck."

"You mean with the bucket?" asked Schlonager.

"With everything. I don't hate you, Honus. It's more like despisement. Or the downright loathsomes."

"Thank you. Stand by to start passing the bucket. Get Pulaski to handle it on the horse end. He's got the best way with them. One bucket each. And one for us."

"Six buckets," said Scortini. "I'll stop you if you run over. I know you're all heart and a hard worker."

"Thanks again," said Honus Schlonager, and disappeared down the wolf hole.

The next hour, and each ten minutes of it seeming the full sixty in length, was spent in drawing six buckets of water from the bank hole of the creek, passing them up into the shed and rationing their precious contents among man and beast. The work was exhausting underground, for Schlonager had not only to crawl on his stomach through the thirty-foot oat bin section of the tunnel, but to inch the filled bucket along ahead of him without spilling more than a teacup or two of its needed burden. When he had handed up the final bucketful to Scortini, he stood gasping and panting in the bin, unable, literally, to climb up out of it. Scortini put down the bucket and offered his sinewy clasp to pull him up, but the sergeant shook his head. "Got to go back," he said. "Haven't had time to talk to Mrs. Shuffman yet; something's wrong: I'll check it and be up in a minute. What time is it?"

"What *time* is it?" demanded the other. "*Madre Maria!*"

He pulled out the old tin watch, brushing the sweat away from his eyes to see its crooked hands under the smudged and cracked crystal. "Five P.M. On the nose."

"Good. Plenty of daylight left."

"My God, yes. And who cares?"

"You've got to keep track of the time," said Schlonager. "I'll be back shortly. Keep the bin lid shut now."

"Sure," Scortini called after him. "And, remember, it's important."

"What's important?" growled the big sergeant, halting with his head and shoulders in the tunnel.

"Keeping track of the time. It separates us from the beasts of the field. So just watch your time down there and don't get mixed up with no animals. Especially no female animals. They're the worst, you know."

"I know you're crazy, you Eyetalyan ape. Shut the lid!"

"Sure," grinned Scortini, easing the oat bin closed. "Oh, for the life of a sergeant!"

"Go to hell!" muffled up Schlonager's voice from

below. "Somebody has to do these things!"

Scortini cracked the oat bin lid and leaned down.

"Why not me?" he called after the big sergeant's vanishing rear quarters. "I'm younger and prettier and can get around better in a small place. You're not being fair to your friends, Honus!"

Schlonager heard him, but kept on crawling. It paid to have a thick hide and a plugged ear in the Cavalry. He well knew what the corporal was firing at, and what the other men up in the shed would be talking about every minute he was underground with the woman. He couldn't help that. It was the one thing men would talk about right up to the side of the coffin, and then be still hollering about when the lid came down on top of them. So let them leer and grin, or curse and scowl, up there in the shed. He knew his own mind and purpose; it was only to see what the trouble was in the wolf den and then to calm down the widow and her babes and to find out, in between, why she, the mother of the brood, had not gotten into Shank's uniform and come back up to the shed, as she had started to do an hour and more, gone. That was all. There wasn't another thought in his hard German head. Not then, God knew. Not with all the other worries Honus Schlonager had to straighten out before the sun went down and the Sioux came for the stock shed.

He nodded to himself in the dark throat of the tunnel, satisfied with his reassurances to himself. Ahead, now, he could see the glimmer of the candle in the denning room. For some reason its small beacon warmed him greatly, and he crawled on with eagerness and anticipation not precisely in the mold of a man going to investigate trouble and woe. The ardor proved factitious. The original instinct was the correct one. There *was* trouble in the Shuffman brood. It was the sickly baby girl.

"She's sleeping now," said Dulcie Shuffman, "but she's so weak, so very weak . . . I'm feared for her, Sergeant."

Schlonager took the baby and looked at her. It was just something he felt he ought to do, there wasn't any real sense in it. "I can't tell, Ma'am," he said, handing the child back. "She's such a tiny, helpless thing."

They sat watching each other over the candle's light. On the sand at the far side of the den, the two older children lay in fitful slumber, worn out with the long hours of strain, half drugged by the close air of the wolf burrow. Schlonager glanced at them and his companion put her finger to her lips, and he nodded and went back to looking at her. She did not drop her eyes, nor yet was her return study of him in any way bold or suggestive. But there was a hunger in the eyes of both, a long-time loneliness that was melting with each second of the open, sober gazing of the one at the other. Schlonager felt it. Dulcie Shuffman felt it. Both were glad and grateful for its spreading glow; neither was made awkward nor hesitant by it; each was content to sit there and to let it grow within them, knowing full well where it would lead if one of them did not stop it. It was the woman, finally, who reached out and put her fingers deftly to the candle's tallowed wick, bringing the darkness and herself to Honus Schlonager.

24

THEY CAME AT SUNSET, RATHER THAN AT DUSK. THERE was no attempt at deception or surprise. They began filtering into position around the shed just as the sun sat on the sharp spires of the Tetons and seemed to hesitate at the touch, before settling farther. By the time the red-orange burst had been halved by the ragged spine of the main range and the shadows lay black and purple out over the Targhee Forest to the Gros Ventre peaks and the treeless portals of Green River Pass, the dark bull pines of Shuffman Meadow and the aspen and willow of Gooseberry Creek were filled, three sides around, with mounted and nervous horsemen of the combined Sioux force. When the last chip of the sun winked out over distant Yellowstone and the sky flamed scarlet-blue behind Washakie's Needles and the Red Tops, Little Killer shouted the Sioux courage word *"H'g'un!"* and the Indian horsemen swept out of the pines and the aspens and the willows, down upon the tiny stock shed.

From force of Indian fighting habit, Schlonager picked up the little Sioux in the sight of his carbine. Get down their leader and they don't like it, was an axiom taught every recruit east of Salt Lake and west of Dodge City. It was like chopping off the head of a poisonous snake. The main body might writhe and threaten for some time but it was blind and not dangerous. Yet the big sergeant could not squeeze the trigger on Little Killer, and he let the sights slide to a hawk-faced Hunkpapa riding to his right, and he killed him with a bullet through the throat at forty yards.

On Schlonager's right side in the open shed front stood Mario Scortini, and on his left side Casimir Pulaski braced his Spencer and fired methodically. Squint Hibbard had the rifle slit commanding the creek, Harry Albion, that overlooking the clearing, inland of the stream. At the rear of the shed, Dulcie Shuffman held the third firing port, waiting to pick up any riders who would slip by the men and seek to pass from creek, inland, or from inland to the water, behind the shed. It was a good posting of his arms by the old sergeant, and he had with him that sunset four men and a brave frontier woman who could shoot and would shoot, right to the last pony jump.

The rifle smoke filled the little shed in seconds. Brass from the Spencers spun through the hot air, banging off the pole walls, littering the dirt floor. Indian lead sang and screeched and whistled through the open front of the low shelter. The bullets plugged into the stout timbers and buried themselves quietly, or, glancing at right angles, screamed like banshees and went whanging off to ricochet around the interior of the little building with crazy, bouncing patterns.

But there were six white carbines firing into that yellow mass of red horsemen, each carbine holding seven shots and each shooter getting off his full seven shots in the scant space of seconds required for the Sioux to spur from inland or streamside timber up to the smoking shed.

It was enough.

Forty-two aimed shots in less than that number of seconds, with seven Indians knocked off their ponies and an untold number hit but still able to hang on and ride free, was a price the Sioux had anticipated but certainly not expected to pay. Moreover, Schlonager, with his unerring eye for the leaders, had shot three of the visiting hostiles of rank. Two were on the ground out there in the grass, the other falling off his mustang back in the shadows of the bull pines, his life running out through the meshing fingers of the two hands that he held pressed to his abdomen while still trying to load and fire his Remington Rolling Block rifle.

Little Killer, who had peeled off with his Salts early in the rush when the Oglala and Hunkpapa began to fall, now called out the quitting word and gathered the surviving warriors about him in the safety of the banked campfires behind the bull-pine grove.

Out in the darkening meadow, five of the seven downed Indians were stirring, groping to brace themselves and stagger to unsteady feet, or simply inch along like broken animals to get away with life still warming their tortured frames. Scortini, ramming a fresh tube of ammunition into the buttstock loading port of his carbine, rasped hoarsely to Schlonager, "Crawlers, damn 'em; don't miss, don't miss!" and shouldered his Spencer. "Hold fire!" roared Schlonager, and knocked up the barrel of the corporal's carbine. The shot went wild through the ceiling and Scortini cursed viciously and for the moment seemed about to turn the gun on Schlonager. "You don't want to kill those poor devils," the big sergeant told him, low voiced. "It's over, Mario. Let them go. Easy, easy. Reload all stations, reload . . ."

Scortini, Latin temper aroused by the shooting, wanted to continue it, but Harry Albion called over sharply from his rifle post, "Watch it, they're coming back!" and before the warning was well out of his mouth he had been hit and hurt badly and the Sioux had swept into the meadow again and come straight at the open front of the shed from the near point of the bull pines.

The totally unexpected maneuver, brought off under cover of the increasing dusk and of Schlonager's Christian mercy to the battlefield casualties of the enemy, was led by a Hunkpapa who was nearly as big as Honus Schlonager and obviously as old to the game. He came within ten feet of taking the shed, and three of his braves actually crashed into the open front and died under the shed roof. Only the fact that the troopers had obeyed automatically the sergeant's order to reload on the Sioux retreat, saved the whites; that, and the last-minute joining of an unlooked-for recruit—Mudcat Clevenger.

The renegade came tottering off his prairie hay pallet begging for a revolver and the chance to help the defense. Schlonager ripped his own Colt free and threw it to him without a second thought. Mudcat dug it out of the dirt, held it in his withered left hand, braced his thin back against the wagon stall partition and killed all three of the Sioux who crashed their mounts inside the building itself. It was the crucial contribution to company survival. In the dead-still drift of the powder smoke through the shed, while the garrison spared talk and reloaded without orders, none there but understood the obligation.

There were equally none there who expected it ever to become a problem. One more rush by the Indians and they were done. The mystery of Mudcat Clevenger's regeneration would be buried with that of Pulaski's wife—and Squint Hibbard's real name on the reward posters of the Texas Panhandle—and Scortini's true status as a bandit assassin among the *Siciliani*—and Harry Albion's actual record with the Limey horse lancers in the Punjab—and Honus Schlonager's boyhood in Waushara County, Wisconsin. But the logic of despair was a white man's logic. It was realistic and hence of no value in an Indian situation. The Sioux had fought their fight for that day. It was they who were done, not the defenders.

It was now too poor a light for useful shooting, or even for determining accurately their casualties. The red horsemen withdrew, and swiftly, taking with them as after their invariable habit and at any added risk, all of their dead and all of their wounded who had fallen to the fire of the soldiers. The only casualty count made in the field that day at the Battle of Shuffman Meadow was the one run by Honus Schlonager and Mario Scortini in the tight moment before their "words" over the ethics of executing the enemy wounded: six, the old soldiers agreed; six for certain, with God alone knew how many others, if any others, down in the second, twilight rush.

Three in the meadow and three in the shed.

Six dead Sioux.

Against nobody down for the white side.

It was a heartening casualty list and it held good for the time it took a tall, powder-grimed English private to stagger over from his post and to salute and say to Schlonager, "Lieutenant Harry Fitzgerald Oakes, deserting again, sir," and then to add, with a wan grin and a private wink for the towering American cavalryman; "Khyber Pass is open, Sergeant . . . carry on!"

Schlonager caught him as he fell.

He was dead in the half minute it took to carry him to Mudcat's hay pallet at the head of the wagon stall.

25

OFF TO THE SOUTH, PAST CROW MANE'S RIDGE, THE lightning ran up into the black sky forking its blue tongues and reforking them into a dazzle of electricity that turned the prairie a garish, ghostly, gaslight color, and marked with its chaining glare the tense faces of the five soldiers crouched in the open front of the shed.

"It's going to come on again," said Squint Hibbard. "God, what a chance to go, when it does!"

"That's right," said Schlonager. "If it comes on like this morning and we had enough horses, they'd never catch us. Not till daylight, anyway."

"Not even then," said Scortini. "A hard storm washes out more than the trail. It takes the starch out of a man. They might not even try to come after us."

Clevenger, sitting silently, a little away from the others, spoke quietly. "What you really think, Schlonager? About making it away by horse? You think it could be brought off under cover of that storm? I been watching her build down there since dark. She'll come on, and soon. I got a feel for weather. Drops will be hitting us in the face before five minutes. Then, she'll open up her gut and drownd us, just like she did this morning."

The woman had gone back down into the wolf tunnel to comfort her older children and to care for the baby. She had not wanted to go, but Schlonager had made her. She had insisted there was nothing to do for the baby, and had wanted to hear what the men would say about their situation. But when the lightning and thunder had begun, they had given Schlonager his excuse and he had ordered her to go down and see to her family. He, and the other men, had thought her attitude toward the sick child was passing strange. Yet they all knew the great stress she had borne for all of the days her husband had been gone in search of medicine, and in the past few hours of their own and the Sioux's arrival at the clearing. She would be more than human and more than woman if she did not show some breaks in her shell by this time.

Schlonager was thinking of her, as Clevenger asked the question about getting away by horse. And he was thinking of her in connection with the renegade's question, too. All of them were thinking of the same thing, he suspected. The only difference would be in the way they were thinking of it. "Well," he answered belatedly, "yes, I do think there's a real chance we could make it with the rain and enough horses. But what's the use of saying that? We've got only the rain."

"We've got five horses," said Squint Hibbard.

They sat and watched the lightning and listened to the thunder. Several minutes passed. Those who had tobacco and pipe or paper left, smoked nervously. Presently, Mudcat put a skinny hand out into the night and said, "There's your first drops." He brought his hand back and licked it to taste the beading rain. "Sweet," he said; "sweet and soft as a woman's lips, or a baby's."

The others looked over at him.

"Coming from you," growled Scortini, "that really tears at my heart. Please stop it, a man can bear only so much. Saint Mudcat! Sweet, he says! Him. Clevenger. Jeezzz!"

"Be still, Mario," said Schlonager. "And stay still."

The corporal fell off into a mutter of Italian endearments which, at least, vented his Latin temperament for the moment. Mudcat, however, moved over and squatted down in the circle of his fellows, and said, still in the odd, humble way he had been using, "I'd like to talk yet a bit, iffen you'll let me." The request seemed addressed to the group, or to any one of its members. Squint Hibbard leaned forward and answered for the rest: "Yeah, go ahead, Mudcat. Talk all you like. Don't mind Wop, here. He don't mean what he says; excepting in Eyetalyan."

"All right," said Clevenger, and sat frowning and watching the storm crowd in from the south, seeking for words and ways to use them to get said what he had to say. When he did begin, it took them all completely off guard.

"I asked about the horse," he said, "and spoke of the woman and the baby being soft, and all, for a reason I had in my mind. When I seen the rain, this idea came to me. If that storm gets up here in time and comes on hard enough after she gets up here, I said in my mind, old Mudcat kin yet get away and not go to that jail in Fort Leavenworth, or to them gallows yonder in Fort McKinney." He paused to wait for a splitting crack of thunder to roll off and die in the pit of the night's blackness. The rain, as he did so, began to come harder. The drops were still big, but all the men could feel the wet splash of them, now, bounding in under the shed's roof. "I thought and thought how

I was to do it," said Mudcat, "with this stump of an arm and only the one shot left in this Colt of the sergeant's, which he was kind enough to give to me when the Sioux come in on us this evening. And then I thought of that little old sick baby down there in the hole, and that poor scairt woman thinking so much of the kid, and all. I always had a mind to work like that. Bad and dark and seeing things to hurt others and not necessarily to do me no good either. But this time it was to do me some good. I seen where I could use that baby. I begun to scheme of ways I could get the woman to bring her up here after it got good and dark and the rain had come on, or was abouten to—like right now."

He waited again, giving them the chance to curse him, but none of them did, and he went on.

"I had that one shot in Schlonager's Colt," he said. "I was going to grab the baby and put the gun to its head and say iffen one of you moved to stop me, I'd pull the trigger. I knowed you all knowed me, and felt I would do it if I said. But maybe you don't know me, and maybe I don't know me, either. When I hearn that lady talking to Schlonager about the baby being too sick to help, and her being so brave, no matter, and wanting to stay up here and sit it out with the men, well, my mind quit on me. My old mind, I mean."

He shook his head, sighing heavily. "This damn arm," he said through his teeth, "hurts like God didn't have nothing else to do, save torture it," he said. Then, bracing himself, "There I was, just pulling the

Colt free of my waistband and going to put it in the woman's back and keep her hostage till one of you went down and come back with the baby, which would be little enough for me to carry under my stump arm, whiles I handled gun and hoss with the other. Yeah, that's when the hoss was going to come in. You was going to unhitch me my pick of the five and help me up on it, all the while I was holding the gun on the baby. God, it makes me sick to think on it, now."

It was a clear opening for some of them to say something, to agree, and disgustedly. But none did.

"That's all," said Clevenger, holding out the Colt to Schlonager. "Here's the gun."

Before the big sergeant could take the weapon, or reply to its offering, the oat-bin lid opened and Dulcie Shuffman called, "Will somebody help me, please; I've got the baby here: we're coming up."

Schlonager went over and took the tiny bundled form, passing it to Scortini, who followed a step behind him, while he leaned down and lifted Dulcie Shuffman to the floor of the stock shed. He didn't ask her a thing, but turned and took the baby from Scortini and walked back to the group in the shed front. He stopped by Mudcat Clevenger, holding the soft small form cradled in his thick arms. The woman came to stand behind him, and then Scortini. It was very still. Only the thunder spoke, muted and uneasy, over beyond the south ridge.

"It would have worked, Mudcat," said Honus

192

Schlonager. "You see, it would have come off right to your measure."

Mudcat nodded and dropped his head, having no words to fill the silence that ensued, nor to say what further was in his twisted mind, if anything, of repentance.

Another soldier, and another survivor, of the Fort Pitchfork patrol, spoke in his place.

"It will still work, Schlonager," said the drawling voice out of the shadows behind Dulcie Shuffman. "If you don't think so, ask the lady what she feels jammed agin her backbone."

"Schlonager—!" pleaded Mudcat's reedy cry, "fer Gawd's sake, look out fer him! He's got your gun. Snatched it right out'n my hand. I couldn't even see who it were . . ."

"That's right, Schlonager," said Squint Hibbard. "I've got the gun and I'll surely use it."

"Dulcie," said Honus Schlonager, "stand still."

"All right, Honus," said the woman.

"Schlonager, don't move!" raged Squint. "I can see you tall agin the shed opening. Damn you, I'll kill her!"

"I'm stopped," said Schlonager. "I was just bringing you the baby."

"I don't want the damned baby. All I need is a horse. Pulaski! Bring me that rangy bay of Lieutenant Gilliam's."

"Sure, sure, I bring him. Good horse." The Pole shuffled off toward the stalls, mumbling and groping his way through the pitch darkness deeper in the shed.

"The rest of you stand still," said Squint. "You, lady, and both you and Scortini, Schlonager. You hear now?"

"Sure," said Schlonager, "we hear."

"Scortini?" said the Texas soldier. "*Scortini . . . !?*"

There was a soft sound, a sound like no other sound in the world of sounds. Muffled and yet sharp. And followed, no, cloaked by, a singular thrusting grunt. Squint sighed and was still. Dulcie Shuffman felt the gun muzzle slip away from her back, heard the thud of the heavy weapon striking the dirt floor. She waited, motionless.

"Squint—?" queried Schlonager tautly.

There was no reply from Squint Hibbard, then or ever. But another voice, tempered and cruel as carbon steel, cut across the darkness.

"He got another ride," said Mario Scortini, "a longer one, and lots quicker. . . ."

26

SCHLONAGER WAS STILL HOLDING THE BABY WHEN Dulcie Shuffman came up to him in the gloom.

"I'll take her now," she said, and Schlonager gave over the child with exaggerated caution. The woman smiled sadly. "There's no need for such care any more," she murmured, low voiced. "There's been none since we came up from the cave." She paused, voice dropping lower still. "I'm going to show her to

Mr. Clevenger, all the same," she said. "I feel somehow, that I ought to do it; that he'd like to know."

She moved away from Schlonager through the darkness to where Mudcat sat crouched and quietly moaning with the pain and sickness that was icy cold within him now. "Mr. Clevenger—" she called to him hesitantly.

Mudcat roused himself. He brought up his bowed head, clenching his rotted teeth, determined to suppress the terminal fear that at last claimed him. "Yes, lady," he answered her, "I'm here."

Dulcie Shuffman sank to the floor beside him.

"I wanted you to know," she said, "that the baby has been dead since early night. I've known all the while that she would die, but I'm glad and grateful that you didn't take her, Mr. Clevenger. It seemed that I ought to tell you that." She waited a moment, then said, "Would you like to see her?"

Mudcat looked at the woman, and then at the small bundle she held toward him.

"Yes," he said, "if you're sure it's all right, lady."

Dulcie nodded, and gave the child to him. He took it and held it gingerly, patting it and peering down into its small, still features.

"I think she's smiling kind of," he mumbled. "My, isn't she a pretty little old thing, though?" He gave the baby back to its mother as solicitously as though it yet breathed and had life. "I thank you, lady," he said slowly, "and I want you to know something, too.

195

I'm greatly at peace with myself, the same as you are, that I didn't harm the little girl. I feel like you do, lady; least I believe sorely that I do; and hope to God that I do . . . ."

She did not reply, only put her cool hand to his shoulder lightly and quickly. He whispered hoarsely, again, "Thank you, lady," but did not move to get up and join the other troopers, now gathering once more about Schlonager. After his fellow soldiers had drifted away, however, and when he was certain they were intent on their talk with the tough old sergeant, he did move. He came stealthily to his knees and began feeling along the dirt floor where he knew the body of Squint Hibbard lay with Scortini's knife still buried in it. But it was not the knife he sought. His groping fingers, so weak from the cold sickness within him that he could scarcely command them, closed presently about that which they did seek—the oiled walnut butt of Schlonager's forgotten revolver.

Clevenger raised the weapon, steadying it and steadying himself for what he must do with the gun to save himself in this last opportunity. His body was of ice, now, to the waist, and beyond. Soon he would not be able to make the hand move, would not be able to force it, with the sergeant's revolver, to do his will.

God! but he was sick. And scared. Deadly scared.

He waited another, last minute, listening to the talk by the shed opening. He caught only fragmented bits and pieces of it. The rain had commenced to beat down in earnest, muffling the words of his fellows, cloaking them in softness and warm splashings which were good to hear, and which Clevenger knew would be a great boon to any chance of escape from the hostile Sioux. It was, typically, Mario Scortini's cheerful Sicilian optimism that came most clearly to him in that final, lengthening remembrance of his fellow cavalrymen there in the rain-shrouded blackness of the Shuffman stock shed.

"Well . . . by God . . ." came the scattered phrases of the little corporal's comments, "it looks as though . . . we were getting . . . getting closer to it all the time, now. If the damn lightning will . . . will strike one of us . . . in the thick skull, right quick, we would . . . we would have . . . have enough horses to go around. You hear me, Honus? What . . . what . . . the . . . hell you say to that?"

Mudcat did not hear the big sergeant's answer to the corporal's cynical question, nor did he wait to do so. He had an answer to that question himself. Or thought it was an answer. And prayed that it was.

Mudcat Clevenger smiled.

His arm did not hurt nearly so fiercely now. The cold sickness was gone and in its place he felt a strange good way he had never known in his life before that moment. It was a remarkable and fine thing to have friends, and to be able to help them instead of harming them. To heal them rather than to hate them. To cherish them and look out for them rather than destroy them. Mudcat's smile softened. Surely he was an uncommonly grateful man and, to the limit of his ability to entertain that reward of the spirit known only to the damned and the redeemed, Mudcat Clevenger was also quite likely a happy man when he put the muzzle of Schlonager's Colt into his mouth and blew out the top of his head.

27

THEY WORKED BY LIGHTNING FLASH, AND GROPINGLY. Now that there was a chance to go, Marybell and Huff riding double on Lieutenant Gilliam's powerful bay, they were placed under a fevered haste. The rain, which was their covering artillery, could cut off as suddenly as it had set in. There was no gaging it, Schlonager knew. The Sioux, if they had the obvious escape routes posted, could be gotten past only if the downpour and driving wind held at their present force. He looked out. So far, so good. The water was nearly as dense as buffalo grass. The wind was switching by the minute, turning west and north, and blowing the sheets of rain with nearly flat, whipping gusts that blinded the eye and blocked the breath.

"Let's go, let's go," he called, helping Huff up behind the older girl on the steady bay, "get these horses in line and roped together. Mario."

"Here."

"You got Mrs. Shuffman up?"

"Yes. I give her the iron gray."

"Good. I can see you now. Bring her up here and

put her in line between me and the kids. Pulaski? You got my horse?"

"Yes sir. He's good. Feels strong. The rain, it makes them feel strong."

The men worked in swift silence, putting the horses in line as best they could within the cramping confines of the shed. It was chancy work but the cavalry mounts held to their hard training. They stood like rocks and if moved, moved carefully as cats. In all of the fifteen strained and straining minutes that it required to get them tied together with the staking ropes and in the proper order so that the line could uncoil out of the shed behind Schlonager, no one was bumped, squeezed or stepped on and when, at last, the big sergeant called out, "All set?" and Scortini answered him, "Sure, here's to a happy honeymoon," and the squat Pole rumbled, "I like the rain, it makes the horse strong," there were three Pony Soldiers of Old Wyoming with equal cause to bless the brains and temperament of the United States Cavalry horse.

The obligation was only beginning, Schlonager realized.

Ahead lay fifty miles of stormy night, guessed-at-trails, swollen streams, uncertain directions and destinations. If all went the very best for them, they could hope to put behind them by daybreak some half the distance to Fort Pitchfork, be in long sight of the Cottonwood Rocks and of the good chance that Captain Hobart would have a troop out looking for them somewhere near that landmark, and consequently that they could effect the juncture of troops in the field and so return to the fort in a manner owed to embattled heroes such as themselves. The other way lay blunders in the rainy darkness, the ever-present and even probable injury of some mount in a fall, or simply of coming up with a stone bruise or cut frog or bad quarter-crack that would lame as surely and disastrously as the worst slip and full fall, the quite possible short duration of the rain, the early rising of the Sioux, the lucky guess on the latter's part at the direction of their flight, a hard ride to intercept and cut them off from the fort—there was no end to the elements of the "other way," and Schlonager put it out of his mind and gathered the reins of Chancellor Bismarck, his sixteen-hand roan gelding, and said softly to the waiting animal, "All right, hammerhead, let's go . . ."

The way was down the Big Horn on the Greybull Trail to the point where the Cottonwood Creek branch of the Big Horn came in off the western prairie. Here, Schlonager turned up the Cottonwood's south bank, following the stream west by north. They were nine miles from Shuffman's Meadow at the turn. Minutes later, when the sergeant halted his little column and asked Scortini for the time, he was told, with suitable under-breath profanity and after three failures to light a match in the whooping wind and rain, to take the next fork left, to Hades, and forthwith and forever to tell his own time. With the instructions, the Sicilian corporal handed over the battered pocket watch and said, "Sergeant Schlonager, your grateful men salute you. As a small token of our esteem we would like to present you with this genuine imitation German tin watch. Wear it in good health and go to hell."

Schlonager took the watch, not returning the badinage. He admired his corporal's nervous system but he did not share Scortini's Latin indifference to their remaining dangers. He found his own matches and succeeded in getting one to light. He had no sooner cupped the tiny flame and brought the watch to it, than its donor said brightly, "What time is it?"

The sergeant put the watch away. "It's time to go," he said, "unrope the horses."

They had come all the way down the Big Horn with the mounts still tied together by the staking ropes. The maneuver had been sure but far too slow. It was midnight, and they had made less than three miles in each of the hours elapsed since leaving the stock shed. In the fog and blindly heavy rain of the river-bottom trail the roping of the horses had been a considered risk by Schlonager. Now they could no longer afford such luxuries of safety. The storm was patently thinning away. In minutes, with the inland trail going every mile higher in elevation, they would be able to push their mounts to greater speed. To do this would require individual freedom for each rider. Also, the roughening, rocky nature of the terrain would demand horsemanship as well as good luck if they were to improve on the time they had made so far.

The latter thought plagued Schlonager as he worked with Scortini and Pulaski getting the staking ropes off the animals. If they did *not* improve their speed, daylight would find them too far on the Big Horn side of Cottonwood Rocks. It would give the Sioux too much of a chance to spy them out and ride them down. And as to that chance, there was now in the big sergeant's mind no remaining question of its reality. Back at the Shuffman Meadow, the luck of the trail had played them as foul as even the oldest soldier could accept. It had been one of those crazy things that simply can't happen, but do; the sort of thing that has made kings of corporals and corpses of kingmakers since military history had been written. Thinking of the pure frustration of it now, Honus Schlonager cursed softly and with a vehemence that carried to his fellow N.C.O. Scortini came over to him, his grin given away even in the darkness by the white flash of his teeth. "Was that you, Honus? Tut, tut, there's ladies present," he chided. "They're wet ladies and wore-out ones, I'll admit, but they're the best we've got, and we must see to it that they're properly treated."

Schlonager coiled the last rope. He nodded, lowering his voice. "Our ladies is precisely what I was thinking about, Mario. Damn the luck! Why couldn't we have made it clean away? Another hundred yards, another few feet in one direction or the other, even a matter of thirty seconds, long or short, and they never would have seen us. Now, God knows what'll happen."

"Well," said Scortini, "us and God."

"It's what I mean," groaned Schlonager. "They're as apt to be ahead of us as behind us, now. True, they don't like riding at night. But they won't have to do that, damn it. All they have to do now is be ready to go with first light. The rain is pulling off north and by four o'clock they'll have seeing light and by six o'clock, full sunrise, they could be as near the rocks as us. They've got a straighter trail and a shorter one going the Gooseberry route. If they leave at four . . ."

Scortini scowled unhappily. "Well, if you want to be gloomy about it," he said, "allow me to add some yet more cheerful thoughts. When that freak wind blew clear that spot we rode into just leaving the meadow, and that mangy Hunkpapa sentry practically had to jump to keep from being rode down by us, we might as well have surrendered right there. Those redguts know we can go only two ways—down the river for Greybull, or back west to Pitchfork. All they got to do is send a party along both tracks and our hair is as good as drying in the breeze their ponies will fan up running for Canada and the border."

"I know," said Schlonager, "and there's more: those new Indians, the ones that rode in from Crazy Horse's camp, are reservation jumpers. I know that big son leading them. He's a brother-in-law of Gall's. A bad Indian, name of Iron Face. He and his bunch have been around the whites too close and too long. They're not apt to be bothered by the old taboos so much as Little Killer and the Salts."

"Such as what old taboos?" asked Scortini hesitantly.

"Such as old taboos about not riding at night," answered Schlonager. "It's my guess that he and his Hunkpapas and outlaw Oglalas will be moving as soon as the rain lets up."

"There's still the chance we'll get to deal with the Salts—that the others will go down the Big Horn to Greybull."

"No, that's not the chance, Mario. I figure old Little Killer to quit and go home. He's one of the original kind. I know them. He'll have counted those dead up there today and then he'll balance them against what he's killed of us and he'll come out with six for them and six for us, and he'll call it a raid and cut for Canada."

"Well, hell, that's all the better, ain't it?"

"Yes and no. Yes if Iron Face takes the Greybull trail, no if he takes the Pitchfork road."

"That's the chance, eh? Hell, it ain't a bad one, Honus. You got to gamble sometimes."

"You do," said Schlonager, "and that's just the trouble. Those Hunkpapa are the greatest gamblers you will ever find to bet against. They'll try anything, and do it for nothing. They just plain like to take chances. It's the best thing they do."

Scortini nodded soberly, then shrugged and grinned. "The hell with it," he said. "Let's put our money on the line, Honus. I feel lucky; come on."

Schlonager sighed heavily and turned with his

friend to mount up. "Well," he muttered, "there's still one thing certain, anyway."

"Yeah?" said the cynical corporal, "what's that?"

"You never can tell," answered Schlonager, and swung up on his stout roan and waved the little cavalcade once more forward.

28

SCHLONAGER WAS CORRECT IN HIS LAST ESTIMATE TO Corporal Scortini, and the Hunkpapa were the best gamblers on the prairie. When day broke clear and hot after a drying wind had blown from the south all night, there were the outlaw Sioux of Iron Face off two miles to the right and riding hard for the Cottonwood Rocks.

The big sergeant estimated the distance that the Indians had to go, against that remaining between his own party and the stone outcropping where he had hoped to fort-up if pressed by the Hunkpapa. Now he would do well to get to the rocks ahead of the enemy, much less having time to dig in and get ready to defend the position and the lives of the settler brood he had been sent out to bring in. Still, he believed that his long-limbed cavalry horses, in any such flat race, could beat the smaller Indian ponies. It was his spot judgment that the finish would be close, but that the race could be won and, indeed, that it had to be. If he did not try to get into those rocks, he would be left to fight the Sioux from the open grasslands that stretched for miles in all directions, save that of the rocks. It was another of the Hobson's choices he had been offered endlessly on this mission, but he took it as he had taken all the others.

"Mario," he said low-voiced to Scortini, "you and Pulaski bring up the rear. I'll lead. Mrs. Shuffman and the kids in between. Let's go."

He dug his spurs into the old roan, shouting to Dulcie Shuffman and the children to follow him. "It's a race for the rocks, yonder!" he yelled. "We win it and we'll be safe for sure! The Sioux don't like pitched fights!"

It was a lie, of course, and a necessary one, but it did not delude Dulcie Shuffman. Schlonager had meant it for the children, mostly, no doubt hoping she would be aided by it as well. The woman urged her flying mount up beside Schlonager's hammering roan. Behind her, the girl Marybell and the boy Huff clung to their shared mount as if with one, forward-bend body, the animal responding to his double burden with gallant will. Dulcie, looking back, saw that the horse was falling back somewhat despite its courage, but she did not abandon her own drive to reach Schlonager's stirrup. The sergeant, watching all of his little troop between urgings of his own mount, saw her coming up and called out to her, "Easy there, let the horse go his own gait; he'll take you there the best way he can!" Then, with a pride very strange for that dangerous moment with all its unresolved threat to each of their lives, he added hoarsely, "He's Cavalry—!"

The woman nodded, tightening the reins and slowing her mount a beat. "I know!" she called back. "I only wanted him to bring me up with you!"

"Hold him just as he goes," said Schlonager. He raised in the stirrups and waved back at Huff and Marybell. "Fine, just fine! Keep coming. You got him running good. He'll bring you. You're real riders and he's a real horse!"

Both children waved back. Schlonager thought he could see the quick flash of their grins and he hoped that he had, as it would mean they had taken him at his word and believed that the rocks meant safety and that there was no question but what their strong cavalry horses would get them there under the time of the Sioux ponies. A moment later, he actually heard Huff's thin yell and saw the boy sweep off his battered hat and swat the horse with it, and then he knew that he had seen the grins and knew, too, that he had, somehow, to make good on his promises that had brought hopeful smiles to the dirty faces of the Shuffman youngsters. His blunt jaw was set hard as base rock when he eased back into the saddle and spoke to the old roan to let out another notch, if he had it. The horse responded, finding the added speed and lifting up the other mounts behind him to run with him in a renewed charge at the Cottonwood Rocks.

Dulcie Shuffman, the wind whipping her light hair in her eyes and mouth, looked over at the Hunkpapa warriors and saw that the race was still entirely undecided, and she called quietly to Schlonager, "Will we make it now, Sergeant?"

Schlonager, in turn, gaged the effort of the Indian ponies against the remaining distance to the rocks.

"Yes," he said. "We're holding them even and those mustangs will give out in another mile. There's a mile and a quarter left to the rocks. We'll make it by two hundred yards."

"Is that enough?" she asked.

"It has to be enough," said Schlonager.

They rode in straining silence, then, the only sounds those of the horses fighting to put every muscle and ounce of will into their running. They had been cavalry trained to go until they dropped, and they were going. Behind Schlonager and the woman, the children's horse was still doing well, and behind him the horses of Scortini and Pulaski drove hard. None of the whites yelled now, not even Huff Shuffman, but across the plain the yelps and cries of the Sioux could be heard for the first time. They carried over the sunlit distance exactly like the yappings and yammerings of a wolf pack in full race, and Dulcie Shuffman shivered and felt weak and was sure, again, that she and her children and the huge, gray-haired sergeant would never get to those rocks. The latter, seeming to sense her thoughts, took his eyes from the Indians long enough to bark at her to ride her horse and quit worrying back at the kids. Everything was going well, he told her. She might even let her horse drop back a little. That would comfort the kids. It would give them the idea that things were not too desperate.

Dulcie Shuffman shook her head, bending yet closer to the tall sergeant as their mounts raced stirrup to stirrup. "No!" she called back to him, "I want to be with you. It's why I came up here. It's my place."

Schlonager felt the thrill of that sink into him and give him the strength of ten. He knew this woman's tough out-country kind. As a breed, these prairie sod-house women were of hickory and blackjack oak. They wore like iron and bent like willow and were harder to break than a Sioux war bow. And this one, he remembered, had already stated her beliefs as to the woman's place in a frontier land and in a fight, or flight, where death was one of the riders always. That place, Schlonager recalled her saying to Scortini, was at her man's side.

He looked at her, squinting to clear the dust and the brightness of the climbing sun from his eyes. He let the roan lean in close to the other horse, and he said to the woman, "Do you mean your place is with me?" and she said, "Yes, I mean that," and both of them rode with their feet and calves touching between the laboring horses and their hearts racing with more than the fear of death, even in the face of death.

"Honus!" shouted Scortini, from the rear. "Look yonder, they're splitting away from the rocks!"

Schlonager saw that what the corporal said was true: the Sioux, having judged the race in their own way and by their own terms, had come to the same conclusion that the cavalry sergeant had come to before them—they knew, suddenly, that they could not beat the white party to Cottonwood Rocks and they had now swerved their lathered mustangs to a sharper angle and one that was figured to strike the line of flight of the fugitives *before* the latter could reach the shelter of the stone ridges.

"Don't veer a foot!" he bellowed to the Sicilian corporal. "We've got the line on those rocks and they know it. All we've got to do is hold it and we'll beat them in. If we give way to their cutting across, they'll have us. You agree?"

Mario Scortini stood in his stirrups, white teeth gleaming in the morning sun. "No!" he yelled. "Let's talk it over a little more. Maybe we could stop up ahead at that level spot where the scrub cedars are bunched and take a company vote on it. Did you bring any beads or knives? We might trade with the natives while we're resting. All right, Sergeant?"

"Sure!" replied Schlonager, and felt better about the race and their chances in it than he had since its beginning. How could you do anything but go down proud with fools like that Sicilian monkey riding your flank? Yet, in another moment, the fleeting uplift of spirit was sent plummeting. The Sioux, having shortened the ground between by their slanting maneuver, began to fire at the fleeing whites as they came on. Schlonager heard the high whining screech of their bullets hurtling overhead seconds before the sounds of the rifle explosions reached his ears. Before either sound, by a split instant, he saw the white cotton bolls of the powder smoke whiffing up from the Sioux ponies centered by the orange bursts of the burned power. He yanked out his Spencer, shouldering it on the gallop. Behind him, he heard the boom of Scortini's carbine, followed by that of Pulaski's, and he shouted to the soldiers to hold low, taking their aim from the over-ranged Sioux fire. Even as he gave the order, one of the Indian ponies leaped sideways and collapsed to the ground, and Scortini yelled back at him, "You shoot your way, I'll shoot mine!" and Schlonager grinned and snugged the Spencer butt into the hollow of his thick shoulder and squeezed off the trigger. Nearly a quarter of a mile away, another of the Indian horses buckled and went down and the big sergeant called back to his corporal, "Don't talk, shoot; it impresses them more!"

Scortini made some insulting reply and even Pulaski, firing methodically, roared something of good spirit in Polish. Indeed, it seemed for that one exciting moment as though their sheerly lucky long shots would turn off the Indians and allow them to reach the rocks in time to dig in for a real defense. But good luck and long shots were not the private property of Pony Soldiers that summer morning. Even as the three cavalrymen cheered themselves onward, a Hunkpapa bullet smashed into the rib cage of the mount bearing the two Shuffman children. The deformed lead veered upward inside the ribs and ruptured the animal's spine near the croup. The brave horse held onto life long enough to slow its momentum and go down without injuring its riders. Then it went limp and died all in the instant it took Scortini to shout the warning to Schlonager.

The latter felt the corporal's cry go through him like an arrow. He very nearly broke the roan's neck hauling him around. Yet swift as he was, his two rear guard soldiers had already slid their mounts to a halt beside the dead animal and were pulling the children up behind them, before the roan could make the turn. It was all done in a scant quarter minute—beautifully, courageously, skillfully, as only old cavalrymen could have done it—yet it was a quarter minute which they did not have to spend. In its brief flight the Sioux had come on with renewed fury.

Schlonager, covering Scortini and Pulaski during the moments of getting the children up, emptied his Spencer into the van of the Hunkpapa, getting down three more ponies and hitting an unknown number of riders. Dulcie Shuffman, belatedly halting her mount, also emptied her carbine into the yelling warriors. The Indians seemed only to come on the more recklessly and clamorously.

Again the idea of the wolf pack came to Dulcie Shuffman. Cold panic touched her. It was an idea, taken in the frightening context of its wild Sioux war cries and gutturally shouted Hunkpapa blood threats, that bore every mark of cruel reality. There *was* an unnerving similarity to animal behavior in the savage, pack-howling of the Indian braves. Wounded and enraged, they were now racing in with redoubled effort, and with doubled, if not trebled chances of success in their final surge to come at the halted whites. Yet Honus Schlonager did not appear to turn a solitary gray hair of his round German head, nor to make a single mistake or false move in the face of this new threat to his small band of survivors.

"Let's go!" he shouted to Scortini and Pulaski. "Up front with the both of you. Dulcie," her name slipped out easily, quickly, "you and me will ride the rear guard this trip." The horses were moving into position, all in place and all getting back on racing stride once more. When they had steadied out a hundred yards or so, Schlonager again called over to Dulcie Shuffman, "Can you load the carbine and watch your horse, too, Ma'am? If so, we'll do a better job of holding back those devils so the kids can be gotten under cover. It helps to pinion the weapon under your left arm, butt forward, while you slide in the shells. Try it. Maybe you'll get the hang."

He was riding with her once more knee-and-knee. His talk came with no more agitation than would be caused by being aboard a running horse in any case. She gave him a tight smile. He thought it was an expression of reassurance to him that she could handle the reloading of the Spencer and still stay with her mount. It was actually a grimace of wry amusement produced by the fact that he was already back to calling her "Ma'am," and had apparently not realized the "Dulcie" had popped out under pressure.

"I'll get the hang of it, Sergeant," she replied, pinning the empty carbine with her left upper arm, showing a natural skill few recruits could boast. "Somehow, you give a body confidence. A woman can do remarkable things with the right man." Then, getting the last of the shiny brass rounds safely into the buttstock loading tube of the Spencer, her gray eyes steadied and she swung the weapon to the ready. "*Now,* we will make it, Honus," she called tersely to Schlonager.

His sunburned features tightened. He seemed to sit a full foot taller on the galloping roan. He brought up his own Spencer, levering it quickly.

"We'll make it, Dulcie," he answered, "you and me together," and began firing, with her, low and straight, into the nearest of the red enemy.

29

IT WAS WHEN THEY WERE WITHIN THE LAST SIX HUNDRED yards of the race that Schlonager saw they were going to lose it; the Sioux had gained too much in the pause to pick up Huff and Marybell Shuffman. The red horsemen had quit firing now, because they could see as well as the old sergeant that they were going to be first to the Cottonwood Rocks. There was no longer any reason to keep shooting and thus injuring any more of those fine big cavalry horses, which were so prized on the north plains. The Sioux, accordingly, had sheared off once more and were riding a parallel course to that of the fugitives, but nearer the boulder-studded refuge looming ahead. Now they had "the angle" on the common target, and they knew it. As Schlonager realized this, another disaster threatened—he saw Pulaski's horse appear to falter, and begin to give ground to the others. In another moment, the Pole's mount had dropped clear back to a point just even with those of Schlonager and Dulcie Shuffman. "The horse is quitting!" shouted the squat coal miner. "He won't run any more carrying double. Here—!" he swept Huff Shuffman out from behind his saddle, handing him over to Honus Schlonager before the big sergeant could move to question the maneuver. "You take him," growled Pulaski in his graveled accent, "I got to look after myself!"

Surprised that the Polack trooper had at last shown fear, Schlonager nonetheless took the sod-house boy under one arm, waved with the free hand to Pulaski and yelled that he understood and agreed with the strategy. It was a military fact, too, that he did agree. It was better to have the Pole stay with them—to have his carbine stay where it would count at the finish— than to lose him *and* his Spencer, just to prove that he was a hero by keeping the boy with him on his failing mount and thus costing two lives and one gun, in entire vain.

"We can still make it!" he called to Pulaski. "All you got to do is keep up another quarter mile. Can you go it, you think?"

He saw the Pole look at him in his dumb, staring

way. Then he saw that quick, strange twist of his broad features which he had seen once before, and called a smile.

"You damn poor liar!" said Casimir Pulaski, and turned his slowing horse aside from the course of the white party and drove him, with the animal's and with his own last strength, directly into the path of the closing Hunkpapa.

Too late, Schlonager saw the purpose of the slow-minded trooper's sacrifice. The Pole's horse responded to its rider's yells and spurrings in a manner that showed that it had not failed, at all, but had been held down and brought back to Schlonager's place at the rear of the party with a deliberate hand. The animal went on a flat gallop toward the Sioux, and with such a burst of final speed as to bring it and its rider across the line of Indian approach to the rocks, before the startled redmen could appreciate the sheer audacity of the cavalryman's intention. In their astonishment, they instinctively slowed their own forward rush for a breath or two. It was all the time that Pulaski had bargained for, or needed. Inside the instant, he had thrown his lathered mount off its feet from the full gallop and, as the creature fell heavily to its side, he was prone behind it in the standard cavalry "open country" fire position. When his carbine began to boom, the Indian ponies were into point-blank range. The seven shots from his heavy-caliber weapon drove into the packed ranks of the red horsemen with the demoralizing force of thunderbolts. Neither riders nor mounts could stand to such punishment. The Hunkpapa ranks parted and veered off to the left of the rocks, but in passing the lone white rifleman they poured in upon him a veritable blizzard of Winchester fire intermixed with war arrows and even some hurled buffalo lances. It was one of the latter, thrown by Iron Face himself, that struck Pulaski in the throat, ranged downward through his loyal heart and drove the life from him in the time required for the Sioux leader to slide his pot-bellied mustang to its hocks, whirl the little animal about, and begin shouting for his followers to rally on him, and to return to the race for the Cottonwood Rocks and the scalps of the fleeing whites.

But his rallying cry was too late, and Sergeant Honus Schlonager had his desperate band over the finish line and into the rocks by one hundred yards. He was already shouting his orders to its members to "fire slow, fire low," when Iron Face and his fellows came at them in the final charge.

The fate of the Pitchfork Patrol at this point became academic. Schlonager and Scortini, and very likely Dulcie Shuffman as well, certainly understood that simply having won the race to the rocks did not guarantee them anything save the chance to die fighting—to take a few of the red devils with them—but this was enough for brave men and women. It was the chance to live another five minutes. Or fifteen seconds. And God alone knew what could or would happen within such time to alter the futures of two old cavalry soldiers, one faded blonde sod-house woman, and two dirt-smeared, prairie-rat white kids. What did happen, in fact, was no less a miracle than Schlonager winning his party's way to the Cottonwood Rocks, and it was no less the result of blind luck and those other factors of survival in a harsh land which in no degree depend upon, or operate under, normal stresses and circumstances.

The white fugitives had flung themselves into the first, lower rocks of the stony ridges of the notorious ambushing place with no time to examine their sanctuary for other occupants. Their sole thought was to get under cover and commence firing. Hence, they were no more prepared for the crash of rifle fire that greeted the galloping Sioux warriors, than were those stunned braves, themselves.

All that they knew is what Iron Face and his two score Hunkpapa renegades ran into as they drove their runted ponies eagerly into the lower rocks on the heels of the old sergeant and his party; and what they ran into was a deadly ambushing by United States cavalrymen, dismounted, among the higher rocks of the trap. From the roaring and booming of the big Spencers reverberating in such narrowed quarters, the startled Sioux assumed they had blundered into the most wickedly outnumbered killing of high plains Indians since Colonel Ranald Mackenzie had caught the Cheyenne of Dull Knife and Wild Hog in the November Big Horn Mountain Massacre of the prior year. The fortunate survivors, thirty-nine in all, began throwing down their rifles among the rocks and yelling up to the Pony Soldiers behind Schlonager's party to take pity upon them. They soon literally stood with their hands upraised in shocked defeat and calling out frantically, *"That's enough, that's enough! you have caught us and we will come in peaceably!"*

They meant, by the promise, that they thought they had run into a full regiment of cavalry, in the field for the express purpose of running down the Crazy Horse fugitives, of which outlawed band they were of course a guilty part. And that, moreover, they were surrendering to this superior force with war honors and were expecting, thereby, to be conducted to Fort Robinson, Nebraska, and made full military prisoners like their great fighting chief before them, and also, by that token, heroes to their own people in the same way that he, Crazy Horse, was.

When, very shortly, they found out it was only Captain Hobart and twenty-two troopers from nearby Fort Pitchfork, in Wyoming, they offered to fight again if the Pony Soldier Chief would only return their guns to them and give them back their horses to ride. But Captain Hobart was an old professional soldier and no friend to the red man. All that he did was to make Iron Face and his outraged braves walk on foot all the way back to Fort Pitchfork, the severest possible indignity to the bowlegged, haughty Sioux horsemen. The incident marked the end of an Indian era in that land, as well as the beginning of a cavalry legend to replace it, neither of which events was precisely evident to its principal actors at the time.

The red captives were subsequently shipped away to the Indian prison camps over in the "dry country," the various established reservations in the two Dakotas to the east, and the army wanted to give Honus Schlonager a lieutenancy for bringing them in and it did make Captain Hobart a major for his part in the *"dangerous and incalculably daring feat,"* which, according to the later legend engraved on granite near the Cottonwood Rocks, *"broke the back of Indian resistance on the North Plains for all time."*

But the army was not quick enough for Honus Schlonager.

The ponderous German noncom was not interested in advancing his military career. Quite to the opposite, he insisted that he would stay at Fort Pitchfork and in the uniform of dark blue and bright gold which he had worn to work for twenty-three years, eleven months, thirty and a half days, only as long as sundown of that same August 3rd, 1877, when his present regular enlistment expired.

Like everything else that Schlonager said, he meant it to the dot of the period.

Exactly as the sun was sinking below the rim of the far Tetons, and the long black shadows of the Targhee Forest were running out to the bases of the Gros Ventres and the portals of Green River Pass, Schlonager set out from Fort Pitchfork in an old ammunition wagon with a team of artillery mules purchased legally from the post sutler. Tied haphazardly to the creaking tail gate were a ribby milk cow and the old roan gelding, Chancellor Bismarck. The cow was the gift of his fellow enlisted men at Fort Pitchfork, the gelding the grateful and official "presentation" of the United States Cavalry itself. In the hay-filled bed of the wagon slept the two bone-weary Shuffman children and upon its rickety seat, proud and quiet and hand in hand with the old sergeant, sat Dulcie Shuffman.

His destination, Schlonager had said, was to drive the woman and her two kids back to the Gooseberry Creek homestead to pick up a few things and head on West.

It may have been so, or it may not.

His soldier friends at Pitchfork were never to know.

For the fact of the legendary sergeant's farewell to the lonely frontier garrison was simply this: from the darkening hour at Fort Pitchfork when that final August sunset closed its mysterious twilight aura about him, Honus Schlonager was never seen again in Old Wyoming. . . .

The rest is the mellowed part of the legend; the part that is suitable for state highway departments to chisel into tasteless pieces of granite which they surround with quaint frames of lodgepole pine and erect in obscure roadside turnouts that no tourist ever stops to visit, but where the restless wind occasionally pauses to pray at the rock and laugh softly at the stuffy words which are about as true as the rest of the advertisements along the concrete ribbon, only not nearly so interesting to the whizzing motorist who knows the nutritional superiority of a greasy hamburger to a state historical marker. But the record has got to be respected. And so these details herein given, along with some others added later to fill in the dull spots are, in the main, the Old Wyoming bones of the Sergeant Schlonager legend. These bones may still be heard to rattle out there in that country of a quiet summer evening, or a cracking cold winter one, if the dude listener is polite, tongue-tied, impervious to detours along the storyteller's way, and neither slow nor reluctant to put another piece of silver upon the bar while waiting.

Schlonager remains a name out there to mention with Terry, Gibbon, Miles, Custer or Mackenzie, and that is a passing strange thing, too. For all he ever actually did to earn the gold leaf of regional gilding for his homely face and hulking form was to go out and bring in a sod-house widow woman and her shaggy-haired kids—something any grizzled cavalry sergeant worth his three stripes could have done, and likely with a lot less of loss and trouble than old Honus Schlonager.

The difference was that Schlonager had the Midas touch for being remembered; he knew when to disappear.

That, of course, is the real reason why they still say of him out there what they do: *that it took a mighty tall horse to carry him.*